THE PORTAL

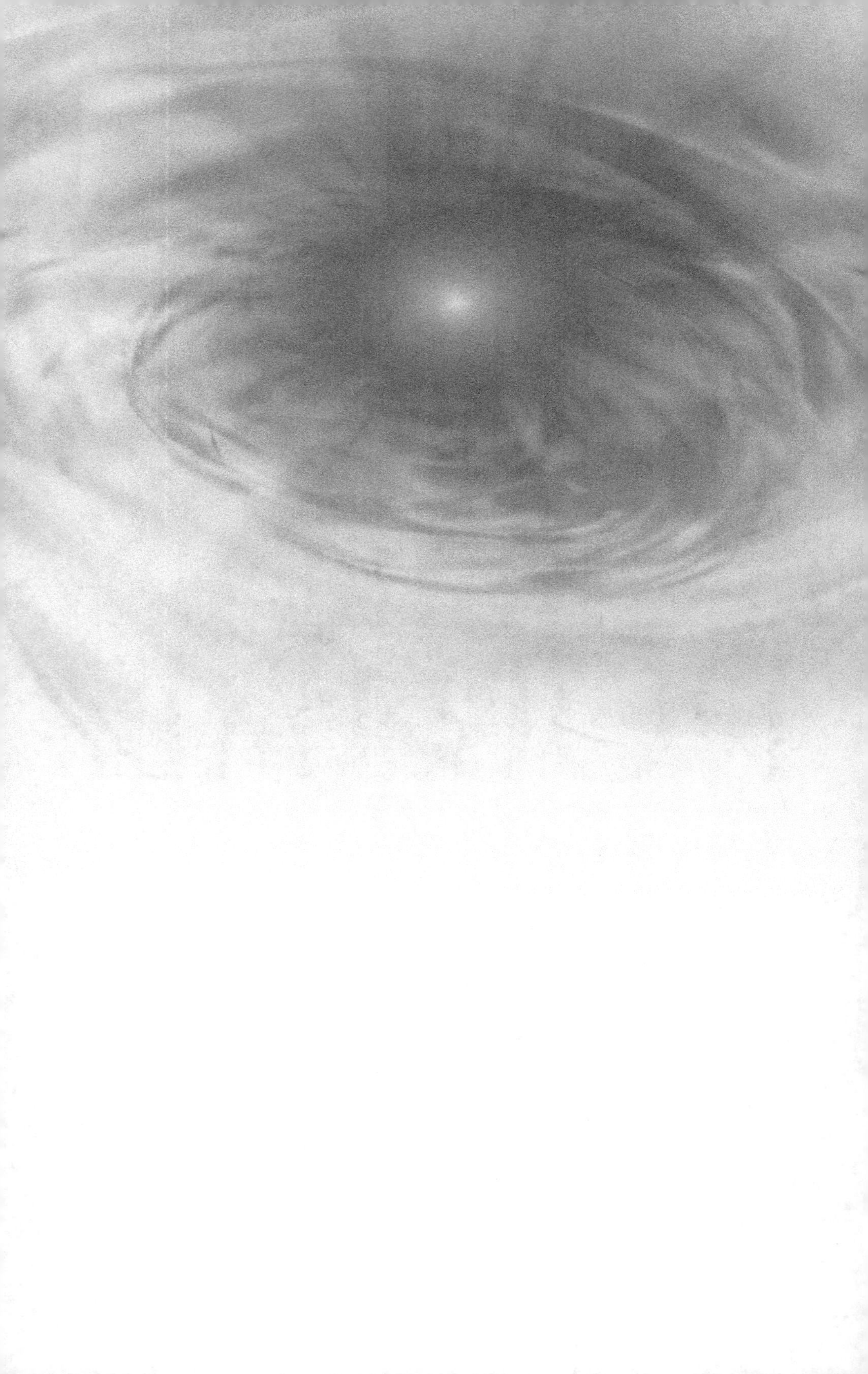

THE PORTAL

LOU PUGLIESE

THE PORTAL

Library of Congress Control Number submitted Jan 2 2026 case# 1-15068832261

ISBN 979-8-9900726-7-1 (hardcover)
ISBN 979-8-9900726-8-8 (paperback)
ISBN 979-8-9900726-9-5 (e-book)

Book Cover by Chris Holmes
Interior Design by Autumn Skye
Editing by Jennifer Ellen Cook

First edition 2026

'The Portal' is the third entry to the 'Blame it on the Moon' series. Each book is a stand-alone tale with hidden gifts across the award-winning series for those that follow the characters' ongoing journeys. The stories cross genres but all are grounded in the same eclectic ensemble cast of distinctive characters that remain true to themselves and each other, as referenced in the following editorial reviews:

> "What I especially liked about the book was the humanity, kindness, respect, and generosity of all the characters . . . a book that can leave you feeling a bit better about mankind than when you started reading."

> "My favorite part of this book is an unexpected detail: the recurring theme of finding friends in unexpected places resonates deeply . . . And just as in real life, the connections expand and develop from there."

> "The dynamic cast of characters, from Richard to his allies and adversaries, were all characterized by their unique dialogue and attitudes, making them distinct, relatable, and interesting . . . each well-crafted interaction feels empathetic and real."

THE SERIES

'Blame It on the Moon: A Haunted House Mystery'

. . . tells a tale that starts in Arlington Virginia in a house that was a field hospital during the Civil War. It's a gripping blend of paranormal suspense, historical mystery, slow-burn romance, and emotional redemption—perfect for fans of The Haunting of Hill House, The Thirteenth Tale, or Midnight Mass. If you love your ghost stories with atmosphere, emotion, and a cast of unforgettable characters, this one's for you! https://a.co/d/51Qx7Wz

**'Final Exam: The Don Weston
Prequel to Blame it on the Moon'**

. . . brings us to the campus of a small liberal arts college in central Pennsylvania. It delivers gut-punch twists, missing persons, and gruesome deaths that shatter the quiet community. Dark, cerebral, and disturbingly intimate. If you like cozy mysteries, 'Final Exam' may not be for you. If you like crime thrillers that share dark, disturbing details of graphic murder and alternate lifestyles, you've found your next read. For fans of Michael Connelly, Louise Penny, and Tana French. https://a.co/d/4fHjwS5

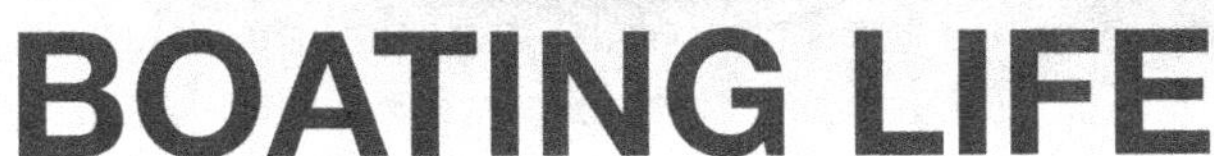

BOATING LIFE

IT WAS A BEAUTIFUL EARLY SUMMER DAY
when Vicki died.

"Captain, may I have permission to board?' shouted Darell as he approached the boat.

"What's the password?" responded Trey Roadcap.

"New York Giants?"

"Good enough," laughed Trey, a retired NFL lineman from the New York team.

"The girls are on their way," said Richard, a friend of Trey's.

Darell asked, "What are the adult plans for today's outing?"

"Just some lazy cruising and maybe some water skiing for a bit. We'll head down to Vola's Dockside Grill in Alexandria a little later for lunch."

"Anything I can do to help get ready?" asked Darell.

"Stay the hell out of the way," Trey said and chuckled. "I already have one landlubber on deck tangling ropes as it is. Richard has been demonstrating that he knows as much about boating as he knows about football."

The girls arrived together after coffee at Richard's house. Richard's wife, Audrey, and Trey's wife, Vicki, were normally barely dressed in the sun with their bikinis on display, but they both went with the more practical one-piece outfits for active wear. Not to mention the cover-up Audrey wore to hide her eight-month pregnancy.

"We don't leave the dock until everyone has a life vest on," announced Captain Trey. "Aye, aye, Captain," laughed Vicki. Vicki was a tiny thing, just over 5' and less than 100 pounds. She laughed that 6'7" Trey didn't know how to swim, but she secretly appreciated his prudent caution. They all suited up and pushed off.

By the time all the boaters arrived, the Potomac would be choppy, but for now, the morning water was calm, perfect for some skiing. Darell was the only guy water skier, and he was fairly new to it, just learning the basics from Vicki in the past few weeks. Both women were quite skilled and daring at the sport. Trey ramped up the throttle, and off they went.

After about twenty minutes of practicing small wake jumping, Darell was ready for a break, and Vicki took over at the rope. Vicki was a slalom skier and loved speed. Her tightest turns dipped almost horizontally to the water, letting a free hand drag the surface. She was also a master of the 360-degree spin, just to show off.

Trey wondered out loud to the rest of the boat crew as they watched the display, "Do you think it's easy because she's so small?"

Vicki was standing on the ski deck reeling in the tow rope when a small boat traveling at high speed cut behind Trey's boat and hit the ski line. The line tangled in its propeller and quickly severed, snapping back to hit Vicki on the side of the head with the force and the sound of a cannon going off. She was already unconscious as her body was launched into the Potomac.

Richard looked to Trey first. Before Trey could finish saying, "I can't swim," Darell was in the water and thinking, *"ABC, airway, breathing, circulation"* from emergency response training. He quickly gathered the inert tiny form. The life vest helped with the dead weight as he rolled her up onto the boat transom and went to work, reciting his thoughts and actions out loud. "Airway," he said as he put Vicki on her side and firmly pressed her back and abdomen. "No water." He stuck his fingers in her mouth, "Airway clear." He gave her a breath to see her lungs inflate, "Airway clear, not breathing, need to start circulation." Vicki hadn't been in the water for sixty seconds before he had already assessed she wasn't breathing. Darell stripped her life vest and rolled it up under her neck to keep the airway open as he straddled her and started compressions while yelling out instructions.

"Trey, head for the marina as fast as you can go. Richard, call 911, tell them Sergeant Darell Metz of the Arlington Police is coming into Columbia Island Marina with an unresponsive female victim with a head injury. Tell them to have an AED at the dock when we arrive. Audrey, grab my shirt and come down here. I need you to hold it on Vicki's head and keep pressure on the wound."

In less than five minutes, which seemed like an hour, they were at the dock to the sound of first responder sirens on the way. The 911 operator had already called the marina staff and they were waiting with the AED. Darell continued compressions until Vicki was wired for the initial shock. Her body thumped loudly on the ski deck as the first charge was delivered. With no immediate response, Darell continued compressions. The AED automatically ramped up the voltage for a second charge, which jolted her again. This time her heart started and Darell was able to assess shallow breathing. He stepped aside for the EMTs to take over for intubation and transport.

Darell hugged a sobbing Trey. "Go with her," he said. "We'll get the dock folks to secure everything here, and we'll meet you at Virginia Hospital Center's Trauma Unit."

VIRGINIA HOSPITAL CENTER

VICKI WAS ALREADY IN THE OPERATING room when Darell, Richard, and Audrey arrived. They found Trey in the waiting room. He was a blubbering mess and they all hugged him. It had only been forty minutes since the accident. Memories and prayers were all they had right now.

Two doctors entered the waiting room. "My name is Paul Cole," said the senior physician. "This is Dr. Flynn, our ICU resident. While Ms. Roadcap is in the ICU, I'm the lead for the care team. I want you to know she is alive and in the best hands possible."

Sighs of relief.

"But we're not out of the woods yet. The final outcome is still uncertain, and the next several days will be a critical time." Quiet sobbing. "Someone administered some remarkable care in response, or we wouldn't have come this far."

"That would be the Arlington County Police, represented by that guy," Richard Craft said, pointing to the shirtless Darell Metz.

Dr. Cole shook Darell's hand, saying, "Ms. Roadcap couldn't have had a better first response if the accident happened right here in this waiting room. Without the immediate attention to blood circulation and the rapid AED application, there would have been no possibility of continued brain function or survival. Right now, we hope to achieve a positive outcome in both."

"Vicki is going to be fine? I'm her husband, Trey."

"We'll know more in the coming days. We anticipate some cerebral edema, or brain swelling. We're going to treat her aggressively to fend off that condition and address what we call burst suppression, reducing any spikes in brain activity that could cause damage or stroke." More quiet sobbing.

"What does that mean?" Trey spoke, trying to choke back tears.

"Her skull was fractured by the impact to her head. We'll be removing a section of the bone to allow release for swelling in her brain. She'll be put into a medically induced coma during the procedure and for the next several days to calm her brain activity. We'll control her breathing and monitor her body's natural responses during that period. She needs to rest."

Trey responded, "Anything it takes. Can I stay with her?"

"No," said Dr. Cole firmly. "I'm asking you to trust us for the next 48 to 72 hours. I promise to personally keep you informed every step of the way. Thanks to your able friend, she never lost brain circulation. Once we get her past the effects of the injury, our planned outcome would be a complete recovery, but we need the next few days to give us the best chances for that."

"Okay," the room went silent until …

"Oh my God," Audrey screamed.

All eyes turned to Audrey as she stood in a puddle of clear liquid still streaming down her legs. "Oh my God," she said again. "I think my water broke."

Dr. Cole calmly said, "Dr. Flynn, call NICU for transport, stat."

"On it," said Dr. Flynn as she left the room.

Dr. Cole went to Audrey. "What is your name?"

"Audrey Craft."

"Audrey, how far along is your pregnancy?"

"Eight months."

"Good. Are you in any pain?"

"No."

"Also good, and what is your relationship to Ms. Roadcap?"

"Vicki and I are like sisters."

"Then I completely understand your stress and your situation. We'll get you quickly to the right medical resources and take good care of you and your baby. I suspect when Vicki is back with us, she'll find herself to be like an aunt."

He turned back to the group. "Are you Audrey's husband?" he said as Richard hugged Audrey and helped her to a chair.

"Yes, Richard Craft."

"Don't be worried, Richard, she's in the right place at the right time. I've met Trey. So, what is the name of our shirtless lifesaver?"

"Darell Metz," he said, extending his hand.

"Trey, Richard, Darell, Audrey. This isn't the best way to meet, but I'm also looking forward to meeting Ms. Roadcap in a few days."

"Vicki," said Audrey. "You'll like her a lot." Smiling now. Dr. Cole's bedside manner had perfectly diffused the tension.

The NICU attendant showed up with a wheelchair. "Hi, my name is Anne," she said, rolling the chair over to Audrey. Anne laughed, "I'm just assuming that the pregnant woman with the wet legs is my patient."

"Good call," Richard laughed. "I'm Richard, and Audrey and I are glad to meet you at this moment."

"Well, Richard and Audrey, glad to meet you as well. I'll be your flight attendant on the next leg of your journey to parenthood."

Audrey stood up to hug Darell and Trey and Dr. Cole with tears in her eyes. "I'm so sorry to be abandoning you guys right now."

"Don't be," said Darell. "We're all happy for you two. Vicki is in good hands with Dr. Cole, and I promise to take care of Trey. Do what you need to do, and we'll all get back together for the birthday party!"

Everyone was smiling with tears in their eyes as Anne headed out with Audrey and Richard.

"Where does that leave us?" asked Darell of Dr. Cole.

"A sort of limbo, I'm afraid. I'd encourage the two of you to stay engaged in as normal a routine as possible while we wait on the next developments. Here's my card with my cell phone number. I'll fill you in regularly on things here, but don't be afraid to call me if you have any concerns. By the way," he said to Darell, laughing. "Can I get you a set of scrubs so you don't have to wander around half-naked all day?"

"I guess I would take a shirt for now. I have extra clothes in the cruiser for later. People would be surprised how often one ends up half-naked in this profession," laughed Darell.

Dr. Cole retrieved a scrub shirt for Darell. "We'll be talking soon. Take care of your business and know that Vicki and Audrey are right where they need to be," were Dr. Cole's last words as he left them to their thoughts.

Trey and Darell wandered up to the NICU to check on Audrey. She and Richard were already in a private room, and Nurse Anne was fixing an IV line to the back of her left hand. They stood outside the door as the attending physician introduced himself.

"I'm Dr. Thibideaux. I guess you're wondering what happens next," he said with a smile.

"Will the baby be okay?" asked Audrey, tears in her eyes.

"I understand you are at least 34 weeks into the pregnancy with no previous complications, so I'm 100% confident that all will go well."

"Good to hear," said Richard, squeezing Audrey's free hand.

"Who is your OB-GYN?"

"Regina Stevenson."

"I know Regina. I'll contact her to let her know what's going on with you and get her on standby for delivery."

"Thanks, I appreciate that."

"I see you have some visitors waiting. I'll let you go for now, but you'll see more than you want of me over the next 24 hours," he said, still smiling.

"What should I be doing?" asked Richard. "Should I plan to stay over?"

"The only thing you need to do is love your wife and your pending child. Tonight, you should probably go home and be as routine as possible. Tomorrow night may be a different story."

Trey and Darell stepped in as the doctor left.

"Sounds like a good plan," said Darell. "How is the mom in the making?"

"Honestly," said Richard. "I'm more worried about Vicki than the mom thing."

"Don't be," said Trey. "Dr. Cole is pretty reassuring about the next few days. Vicki will be back soon. Take care of your situation for now."

"Good news," said Richard.

"We're heading back to the marina to secure things there and pick up Trey's truck," said Darell. "Then he needs to make sure things are good at the gallery. I'm pretty sure I can clear my schedule for the next week and hang loose for whatever any of you need. I'll also stop by and let Lincoln know what's up." Lincoln was Richard and Audrey's sheltie. "We'll be back late afternoon to check on the girls. We can pick you up then to get your car and maybe do pizzas and beer and cigars at your place later?"

"That sounds like exactly what you boys should be doing," said Audrey.

BACK TO THE SCENE OF THE ACCIDENT

DARELL PULLED ON A NEW TOP AS HE AND Trey entered the police cruiser, his last shirt having been relegated to medical waste by the EMTs.

"Darell," said Trey with tears in his eyes. "I'll never be able to repay you for saving Vicki."

With a need to inject some light-heartedness, Darell responded, "Buck up my friend, it's all in a day's work. A couple of beers and a cigar will suit me just fine." Things went quietly for a time as they rode on.

Jay O'Connor, the dockmaster, saw them pull in at the marina parking lot and went to meet them. "Trey," he said. "Is Vicki okay? Is there anything I can do?"

"Not yet, but the doctor told us to be hopeful for a full recovery. Prayers would be good."

"Any word on the other boat?" asked Darell.

"We got the call to tow them in right after you left. They're down at the end of the dock by the service area. Our tech just finished cutting the rope off the prop, and I think they're getting ready to leave."

"Trey," said Darell. "I'm going to have a quick visit with our boating friends while you're wrapping up here."

"Are you going to arrest them?"

"Afraid not. In Virginia and DC, the law recognizes water skiing as an inherently dangerous act. That puts the injury liability on the participant. There's no criminal charge here. That doesn't mean they didn't do anything wrong, and I want to make sure they understand that."

Darell produced his ID as he walked up on two skinny teenagers sitting by the boat. They were maybe fifteen and eighteen years old. "Sergeant Darell Metz of the Arlington County Police Department. Can I get your names?"

"I'm David Douglass, this is my brother Rick." The older one was clearly in charge.

"I understand you had an accident today?"

"Yeah, some dumbasses left a rope in the water, and it fucked up our motor."

"Interesting. I was one of the dumbasses in that other boat." Darell's face was getting warm.

"Then maybe you should pay the bill for the tow and the work on our dad's boat."

"Maybe you should understand the consequences of your actions," responded Darell firmly.

"I didn't do anything wrong."

"See that boat up there at the dock, the one with the ski flag still up? That ski flag was up when you came speeding behind that boat and hit the rope."

"So what, you think I owe you a new rope or something?"

"I think you owe someone an apology for the damage your recklessness caused. Trey, come on down here," yelled Darell.

As the 6'7" Trey started the 100-yard or so walk down the lot from the dock, Darell said to the boys, "That man's name is Trey Roadcap. Thanks to your carelessness, his wife was hit by the rope you cut off. She's now at the trauma center in a coma, missing a piece of her skull."

"Shit," mumbled David Douglass.

"You'd better believe it, shit," Darell said very close to young David. "When he gets here, you're going to give Mr. Roadcap a respectful and genuine heartfelt apology for your part in hurting his wife. Thanks to your selfish recklessness this morning, that man is suffering through the most emotional day of his life."

"Honestly, I didn't know anything else happened."

"Tell him that."

"Is this the other boat?" asked Trey, not telegraphing his feelings.

"Mr. Roadcap, I'm David Douglass," said the older boy. "I heard what happened to your wife. I'm so sorry. I didn't know anyone was hurt. I didn't even know we hit a ski rope until we got towed in here. We were just out having fun in our dad's boat when our motor stopped. I didn't know. I don't know what to say," his voice trailing off.

Darell looked to Trey, not sure what would happen next. No response for long seconds that seemed like minutes.

"Trey?" said Darell.

Trey spoke, "I'm thinking about all the times in my early boating life that I ran over ropes and could have done the same thing. Is your dad's boat okay?"

"I think so, but your wife." David was trembling as what happened began to sink in.

"I know, but I don't think you meant anyone any harm. It was an accident."

"But your wife, is she going to be okay?"

"We won't know for a few days, but I think so."

"I'm so sorry,"

The dockmaster Jay had joined the group. "Jay," asked Trey. "Do you have a pen and something to write on?"

"Sure, what do you need?"

"Get David's phone number for me." Turning to David, "I'll let you know how things turn out."

"What is your wife's name? I'll pray for her."

"Thanks, that helps. Her name is Vicki," said Trey as he and Darell turned to head back up the dock.

They had gone a few yards when younger brother Rick shouted out, "He's sorry he called you a dumbass."

"Keep walking," said Darell to Trey. "He's talking to me. All cops are dumbasses."

Trey and Darell finished packing up the boat so it could be put back in its regular slip.

Jay handed David's phone number to Trey, saying, "Whatever we can do for you and Vicki, let me know."

"Thanks Jay. Would you put the charge for David's tow and repair on my bill? Maybe he won't have to tell Dad right away. We've all been through a lot today, and I'd hate to see a young man lose his boating fun for life after one stupid moment."

"For you, the charge is zero. I'll let the kids know they're good to go."

"Appreciate it. I need to get to the shop and make sure things will be okay there for the next week or two. With any luck, I'll be calling you soon to get Vicki back up on skis."

"Fingers crossed," said Jay.

With a last hug, Darell and Trey parted ways at the dock. "You're a good guy, Trey, things will work out." Darell was going to stop by the office to clear his work schedule for the next week. Trey was heading to the Peacock Plume.

"Darell," Trey yelled as he was approaching his truck.

"Yes."

"Can you teach me how to swim?"

MICHELE AND MICHAEL MILLER

THE PEACOCK PLUME WAS A COMBINATION New Age shop and art gallery that Vicki and Audrey had partnered in launching several years ago. The shop was also home to Vicki and Trey, living in a comfortable apartment on the top floor.

The business stepped up dramatically after some events in the past year, including Audrey's gallery showing her final project for her MFA degree. Audrey's art was in high demand, as was Vicki's following as a paranormal guide. Even with Trey's help, Vicki and Audrey couldn't keep up. They had hired a couple from New England to run the day-to-day customer needs.

Michele and Michael Miller found a serendipitous fit in responding to an ad in an art magazine. They were thrilled as recent retirees to enter the Peacock Plume life. Michele was well-established in her own right as a jewelry artist. Her silver work had a large following. It also included the addition of the gems and crystals that put her and Vicki in synch from their very first meeting.

The Millers also bonded with Trey, as they were rabid football fans. They knew his history well, as his disruptions had contributed to the defeat of their New England Patriots in the 2008 and 2012 Super Bowls.

A red-eyed Trey was greeted with the traditional "Namaste" from Michele as he entered the shop. Trying for normalcy, Trey responded with "Konnichiwa," an inside joke from Richard Craft. "I need your help," said Trey. "I need you to take over the shop for I don't know how long."

"Oh," said Michele. "Vicki was already here with the same message. She said she had some travel that would take you guys away and asked if we could hold things down at the shop on our own for a while. No problem," she said cheerily.

"Vicki was here? When?"

"About an hour ago."

Trey couldn't think. Puzzled, he asked, "How was she dressed?"

"In a swimsuit. She said you and your friends were starting the break with a day on the river."

"That's not possible," said Trey, tears running down his cheeks. "That's not possible."

"Trey, what's wrong?"

"Vicki has been in the hospital for hours. There was an accident on the boat. She couldn't be here. Her skull was fractured in the accident. She's been unconscious since."

"But she was here," Michael said joining the conversation. "We talked to her."

"She's in the hospital in a God damn coma," shouted Trey, breaking down completely.

Michael hugged him first, and Michele joined. "Dear God," murmured Michele as the group hugged. "We feel you with us. Grant us all your healing power for Trey and Vicki and bless these circumstances as growth for all of us in appreciation of your love. In Jesus's name, we pray." Amen from all.

Trey composed himself and said, "Thanks, having the two of you here is a blessing. I know the daily stuff is handled better than I ever could on my own, and I can put all my energy into Vicki's recovery."

"What happened?" asked Michael.

"Vicki was pulling in the ski rope when another boat came by and ran over it. It got cut by the propeller and snapped back to hit her in the head. Fortunately, our friend Darell knew every right thing to do. The doctor says he's optimistic for a full recovery, but the next few days will tell." He paused, then added, "I'm going to lie down for a bit. Darell is coming by in a few hours to take me back to the hospital. Tell him it's okay to wake me if I happen to fall asleep."

"Get some rest," said Michele. "No worries here."

Trey lay down on the bed, but his mind wouldn't stop. *"She couldn't have been here, that couldn't have happened, that's not real. God help me, do I even know what's real now?"*

Trey eventually cried himself to sleep. He saw Vicki in his dreams. "Did you really stop by the shop to see the Millers?"

"Of course, I wanted to be sure you didn't have to worry about it." Vicki was smiling.

"Are you okay?"

"I'm having an incredible journey and experience. I can't wait to tell you all about it!" was the excited response. *"I'll be home in a few days, good as new."*

"Promise?"

"I promise."

"I love you."

"You'd better," Vicki's laughter faded as Trey fell soundly asleep.

"Wakey wakey," yelled Darell as he threw a pillow at the sleeping Trey. "We've got things to do."

Trey stirred and came to quickly. "What time is it?"

"Testosterone time, my friend. I just talked to Richard, and all is well with our girls. I promised Lincoln a real guy's night tonight, some pizza, some beer, some cigars, and some good old-fashioned locker room talk so we can get the weepy behind us and trudge forward as manly men to face our challenges. Get a quick shower, and we'll go find Richard."

Trey was ready in fifteen minutes. A quick goodbye and thanks to Michael and Michele, and they headed back to the hospital.

"Why don't you see if you can touch base with Dr. Cole while we're on our way?" said Darell.

"Good idea."

The doctor answered on the second ring.

"Trey, Vicki is doing well. Everything is going as planned and expected, and she's resting peacefully."

"We're on our way back to the hospital now. Should I stop in to see Vicki?"

"Don't. Trust that all is well here. There's nothing to do for Vicki but let her work on her recovery. I'll have more information for you this time tomorrow."

"Whatever you say, I do trust you. Thanks for everything you're doing."

"That sounded as positive as possible," said Darell.

"It did. Okay, I'm ready to rally for your boys' night debauchery plans. Let's grab Richard and get the party started."

Audrey and Richard were both asleep when they got to the room. Darell had no shame in rousing them with the wakey wakey pillow toss. "Audrey," he said. "I'm taking your husband on the manly version of a baby shower. Your doctor and Vicki's doctor have released all of us until later tomorrow while you two rest. Lincoln said he wants to just hang with the boys tonight. I even got him his own six-pack of O'Doul's."

"You're not giving the dog beer."

"Just kidding, But I did pick up sufficient social lubricant for the rest of us."

"Richard, promise me you won't let Darell give Lincoln any beer."

"Are you kidding? I have to sleep with him. Dog beer farts are not in any of my plans for tonight," said Richard, laughing.

"Then you have my permission to leave your suffering wife in the hospital and go out drinking with the boys."

"I can stay over."

"Not. I need my beauty rest, and you all need to unwind and get ready for the next few days as much as Vicki and I do. Make sure to tell Lincoln what a hero his Uncle Darell was today."

With hugs and kisses, the guys left to pick up Richard's car and headed back to hang out with Lincoln.

TESTOSTERONE TIME

LINCOLN WAS IN HEAVEN, RUNNING BETWEEN Darell and Trey while they had a marathon frisbee event. He snagged every one of their dropped passes to keep the game alive and showed off his best acrobatics when they threw to him. That lasted about thirty minutes until he was spent and lay down in the puddle by the outdoor water pump.

"Me too," said Trey to the dog as he headed in for a fresh beer.

"Pizza will be here in forty minutes," announced Richard. "In honor of Vicki, I ordered all vegetarian."

Trey spit out his first sip of the beer. "Please say you didn't."

"I didn't," said Richard laughing. "I can read the room. Nothing but the meats for this crowd."

"Wings?"

"And cheesy bread. Are you satisfied?"

"Now we're talking."

"Surprise, gentlemen," said Darell. "I set up a Zoom call at 7:00 p.m. with Don Weston. I thought we owed our Pennsylvania constituency an update on today's events."

Don Weston was an old friend of Darell and a new friend of Trey and Richard in the past year. He was the Chief of Police at Churchville University and a Civil War historian. Richard's house was a hospital site during the war. Don and some of his contacts had spent much time there unearthing the past in an archeological dig. In exchange, he surprised Trey and Richard by arranging for Churchville University to pick up the tab for the joint Craft/Roadcap wedding. He'd become more than a good friend to all of them, and the guys agreed they should fill him in on what was happening with Vicki and Audrey.

Pizza arrived on time. The feast was washed down with the first two six-packs of beer.

At 7:00 p.m. the guys gathered around the laptop at the kitchen table to Zoom with Don. When the screen opened, Don was already there with a smile and a cigar. "Now there's a notorious crew," he said. "To what do I owe this welcome summons?" He laughed.

Darell spoke. "Some bad news, Don. We were all out on Trey's boat this morning and Vicki had a skiing accident. She's in the hospital in a coma."

Don's smile faded. "That's very bad news. What's the outlook, Trey?"

"The doctor tells us she has a good chance for a full recovery. We won't know for several days while they keep her sedated."

"Are you okay if I let Abbey know?" Abbey Foster was an archeologist from Penn State. She led the excavation of the Craft property. She also became fast friends with Vicki, bonding over their paranormal interests.

"Please do. I know Vicki would appreciate her thoughts and prayers."

"Abbey will be at the school tomorrow. She's doing more research on the artifacts from the dig. I'll fill her in. Maybe we can come visit when things stabilize."

"We'd like that."

"That's not the only instability here," added Darell. "You want to tell him, Richard?"

"Sure, Audrey's water broke while we were at the hospital. It looks like the baby will be here soon."

"Aren't we a little premature?" Don said, frowning. "How is she doing?"

"She's good. They said she's far enough along for a normal healthy delivery."

"Bad news, good news, I guess. Hopefully, it's all good soon."

"Fingers crossed on all fronts," said Darell. "We thought you'd want to know."

"Thanks for the update. I'll get all the prayer-minded Pennsylvania group engaged."

"Any news in your world?"

"With what you guys are dealing with, I'm embarrassed to say that all is well here."

"Good to hear, we'll let you know how things progress."

"Thanks, let Audrey and Vicki know we're thinking of them."

"Will do."

From the Zoom the evening settled into a couple more six-packs and cigars on the patio. Lincoln relentlessly chased a tennis ball while the men pondered the state of the universe.

"I have to share something," said Trey, slightly inebriated. "I think I'm beginning to believe Vicki's paranormal stuff."

Richard responded, "After the past year's events, I'm certainly less skeptical than I used to be. What's changing your mind?"

"She talked to me while I napped this afternoon. She was really with me. She promised she'd be okay."

"Did you see her?" asked Darell.

"No, but Michael and Michele did. They said she came by the shop an hour before I did to let them know they'd need to handle things on their own for a bit."

"They saw her?"

"That's what they said, I think I believe it. I know they do."

"Thinking with my beer-addled cop head at the moment, I have to ask. Do you have any security cameras we can check online?"

"We do," shouted Trey. "We do! I don't know why I didn't think of that."

They left the cigars on the deck and went to the laptop on the kitchen table. After a little password fumbling, Trey was able to focus on the main counter camera and start scrolling back through the day.

"There I am when I got there from the marina. They said Vicki was there about an hour before that."

Quiet while they rolled back to an hour before.

Clear as could be, there stood Michael and Michele having a seemingly amiable and animated discussion with ... no one.

VICKI

AS A TRUE PARANORMAL BELIEVER, VICKI had long fostered an open-minded wonder around the secrets of the afterlife. While friends and family grieved, she was steeped in the glow of warm and welcome travels.

In her unconscious mind, she was able to see everything in and beyond the real world. When the ski rope hit her, she knew she was dead before she was wet from the murky waters of the Potomac. Instantly catapulted towards a bright light, she knew she was heading to a new world.

She was almost disappointed when she could feel herself slipping backwards as her heart began to beat again. But as long as she hovered between life and death, she hovered between light and Earth in what she knew as the Portal.

Vicki believed that the Portal was that place that all life passed through in its comings and goings between the natural and the supernatural, between spirituality and reality, between arriving and departing. It's the channel we're born from and the place we return to when we die. It's the great equalizer of all mankind.

There is no spoken language in the Portal, but there is a great exchange of sense and thought, of being and knowing. As souls pass, they connect with those being born and those long dead. Some souls linger, others fly past like comets, streaking to the light. While Vicki remained unconscious, not breathing on her own, sedated just below the realm of the living, she played in the Portal. Here she knew everything.

She knew how Darell had worked to bring her back to life. She knew that Audrey would be a new mom in another day or so, and she looked forward to being called "Aunt Vicki." She sought out Michele and Michael with her message to take care, and she snuck into Trey's dream with her message that all would be well. She also wandered up and down the light of the Portal. She visited with old friends, now happy in their spiritual world, and met new ones who were on their way to the physical world.

This place was so positive and energizing. There was one mysterious encounter that she couldn't quite place. It was a very misty apparition of what seemed to be a naked woman. It often floated along with her as if it needed to connect, but they never quite did.

She thought about Trey and Darell and Richard and Audrey and Don and Abbey and everyone else who loved her and prayed for her. She'd have much to share with all of them when she returned.

HOSPITAL DAY TWO

DARELL AND TREY STAYED OVER AT Richard's. They all slept surprisingly well and awoke with little alcohol-induced aftereffects.

Over coffee, breakfast, and another cigar, they planned the coming day. Trey checked in with Michele and Michael and was assured that everything was well at the Peacock Plume. They insisted all of his thoughts and strength should be spent on his wife and good friends while everyone waited on Vicki's return.

Lincoln knew something was not right. He was unusually quiet and moved from hand to hand, keeping close contact with all. He also threw in the occasional zoomies through the house to keep things light. He was a happy guy to have company, but he missed his mom.

"She'll be home soon," said Richard. "And she'll be bringing you a new friend to play with."

Lincoln cocked his head and raised his eyebrows in the universal sign that he understood. He was a good boy, earning extra treats before the group left around noon.

The first stop at the hospital was Dr. Cole. "Welcome gentlemen," he said.

"Any changes overnight?" asked Trey.

"Your wife had two significant activity spikes yesterday in the early afternoon ..."

Trey, triggered and frightened, interrupted him, "Is that bad, will she be okay?"

"Let me start over, I didn't mean to raise an alarm. By *significance* I'm only referring to a degree of relevance on a detectability scale, not a concern or damage exposure event. Patients of concern in this procedure would have hundreds of such events and often suffer differing levels of stroke in the first 24 hours. Even in those cases, we don't rule out a satisfactory recovery. In my 24-hour evaluation of your wife, I'd assess her as the calmest and most promising patient I believe I've ever seen."

"So, she may still be okay after this?"

"I've probably never been more optimistic about a patient prognosis. She has many conditions in her favor. The most critical was the immediate skilled response to her trauma incident. We were presented with a viable, breathing-assisted case and could take intervention in advance of cerebral edema, or brain swelling. Her injury is focal, or limited to one specific area, and not an area of concern for post-traumatic normal functionality. Pupil reactivity has been good from arrival. Her response to the induced coma has been textbook perfect with no seizures. She remains calm in her brain activity and seems at peace with getting the rest she needs and deserves."

"So, she will be fine?"

"If there is no increase in edema, which I don't expect, we'll move to close her cranium by tomorrow evening. The day after we can start to reduce the propofol that is keeping her sedated and bring her back to a conscious level. I anticipate that she'll wake to a headache and some surgical pain and be very happy to see you again."

"Longer term concerns?" asked Darell.

"Not really from my perspective. We'll do a rehab assessment but, because of the injury site, I don't think she'll even require any of the speech or occupational therapy normally associated with traumatic brain injury."

"Thanks, Dr. Cole," said a teary-eyed but happy Trey as he moved in for a big bear hug.

"Then our work here is done," pronounced Darell. "Let us know when you schedule the Frankenstein surgery tomorrow, and we'll be back with popcorn to watch the show. Time to check in on Audrey and her mom journey."

Audrey was sitting in a chair reading when they got to her room.

"You look relaxed," said Richard.

"I am. I got a pretty good night's sleep. There were some minimal intrusions for quick exams and pill taking but I had no problem nodding right off again. I'm also relaxed because Dr. Cole stopped by this morning and said Vicki is doing great."

"We just got the same report from him."

"Now," said Darell. "We just need you to stop procrastinating on your childbirth so all of us can get away from this place sooner than later." He laughed.

"Oh," said Audrey, also laughing, "Didn't they tell you we've decided I'm staying for another month to wait for full-term delivery?"

"Really," said Richard.

"Not really, I couldn't stand that any more than you. Dr. Thibideaux will be here in the next hour to start the process of inducing labor. He says I should be prepared to get uncomfortable in the near future, but by sometime tomorrow all will be well."

"Do you have anything else to read? I thought that was the plan, so I packed some stuff to spend the night. Darell and Trey have moved into our place to hang with Lincoln."

"All sounds good here," said Darell. "Trey and I will leave you bibliophiles to your solitude and pending chaos. We're off on an important secret mission."

MISSION POSSIBLE

THE SECRET MISSION WAS A QUICK STOP TO pick up swimsuits on their way to their inaugural trip to the Alexandria YMCA pool. Arlington Police were using that facility for much of their specialized training as the Arlington Y pools were undergoing renovation. Darell looked in on Kevin, one of the personal trainers at the Y, on their way in.

"Kevin, meet my friend Trey Roadcap, we're going to do some swimming instruction today."

Shaking hands, Kevin laughed out loud and said, "This guy needs no introduction. My wife is a Jersey girl and his biggest fan. I can't tell you how much Trey Roadcap abuse I got over the years as he decimated my Redskins."

"Sorry, not sorry," laughed Trey.

"Trey is a lifetime boater and a lifetime non-swimmer," said Darell. "He's recently become motivated to up his aquatic game, so we're stealing part of your pool to take care of that."

"Happy to be of service. Let me know if there's anything you need."

On the way to the locker room, Trey asked, "Are you sure you can teach me? I've never even been able to float."

"Of course you're not going to float. You've been one dense muscle your entire adult life. But you may have noticed Olympic swimmers are also one dense muscle, and they seem to do okay. You've got everything you need in strength, balance, and natural athletic ability. Once I teach you how to breathe, you'll find yourself swimming today."

"That sounds way too easy."

"It is. You need to learn to be completely relaxed in the water. I know you fear sinking and drowning so, for now, remind yourself you're in a shallow pool and I'm right here beside you. Until you put your mind at ease, you'll be fighting it and messing up your breathing, and you won't make any progress. You've got this. Do you trust me?"

"I trust you," said Trey as they got into the pool.

"Good, we'll start by teaching you how to breathe. You breathe quickly when you inhale and very slowly when you exhale. Keeping the air in your lungs helps your flotation and makes your whole process more efficient. You only inhale when your head is out of the water, for obvious reasons. The part you need to practice is that you'll only exhale when your head is under the water. Once you master that, you'll be a swimmer. We'll have you start with your feet on the bottom of the pool and your hands on the side. I'll call out the instructions while you try it. Ready?"

"Ready."

"Quick deep breath, face in the water, blow bubbles for a five-second count while you're exhaling slowly. Turn your head and breathe again, face in the water, exhale slowly, turn your head and breathe in quickly, head in the water. Keep going three more times." Trey stopped as instructed.

"Well?"

"It's awkward and counter intuitive, but I get why it works."

"We're going to do it again, but this time I want you to step back from the wall. Keep one hand on the side with your arm at full extension and keep the other arm free. When it's time to inhale, do a stroke with the free arm and take your breath on that side. Got it?"

Trey forgot to breathe in on one of the strokes but picked up on the next one okay. Darell had him do ten more.

"We're doing one more addition. Do exactly what you've been doing but let your legs float off the bottom of the pool and flutter kick to keep them up while you're practicing the breathing and one-arm stroke." That was a disaster of sinking and gulping water the first time while Darell laughed at Trey's plight. Trey's competitive spirit and athletic discipline kicked in. He started concentrating more on trusting the process than fearing the drowning, and it came together fairly quickly.

"In the next twenty minutes, you'll be a swimmer. We'll stick with the basic freestyle for now. Once you're comfortable with that you can practice and master any swimming style you want. In the meantime, this is the swim that will save you if you fall out of a boat and the one that will eventually put you in a position to save others.

"Keep your body position flat, your chest on the same plane as the pool bottom. The only thing that changes as you move through the water is the position of your head. Turn it out of the water and take a breath every two to three strokes. Aside from that breath, your face stays underwater at all times. You'll learn what is the most comfortable rhythm for your swimming, and you'll want to keep it consistent. Remember it's shallow water and you can stand up at any time."

There were several minutes of flailing, sinking, choking activities accompanied by Darell's laughter as he kept on calling out *breathe, relax, exhale, relax, extended arms*, and any other instruction as Trey slowly adjusted. Within ten minutes Trey had a working rhythm and Darell let him go on his own. Within twenty minutes, as promised, he was a swimmer. The next lesson was treading water so if his forward momentum were stopped, he didn't risk sinking. With cupped hands and a relaxed manner, he mastered the skill and began to feel genuinely comfortable in the water.

"I knew you could do it," said Darell after they dried off and were heading back to Richard's house. "You take direction well. Now I understand why Vicki likes you."

"That, my friend," said Trey, laughing with him. "Will cost you a steak dinner."

HOSPITAL DAY THREE

TREY AND DARELL GOT THE TEXT AT THE same time. A healthy Elizabeth Victoria Craft joined the world at 3:00 a.m. following a relatively benign labor and an easy delivery. Lincoln was already awake as if he knew the news. The three met in the hall for a high-five and returned to bed.

Darell was up first and made a big breakfast. "We needed another female to balance the group," he said, laughing over coffee.

"Can't have too many females," agreed Trey. "They certainly make life more interesting. Does this make us uncles?"

"I think so. Vicki's going to be surprised and delighted when she gets back."

"I'll say. I wonder if this means she'll want one of her own."

"I'll bet you wouldn't mind if she did."

"I'll just be happy to have her back. Whatever she wants after that is fine with me."

"Let's clean up and go meet the new addition. Little Lincoln sure seems happy this morning."

"I think he knew before we did," laughed Trey.

The first stop was Dr. Cole. "Do you guys ever sleep?" asked Darell.

"Not so you'd notice. We veterans know how to get our rest between visits. Speaking of rest, Vicki had another perfect night. We've scheduled her cranial reconstruction for noon today. If all goes as anticipated, we'll begin to wean her off the propofol in the early morning hours, and she should awake pretty happy and hungry in the mid-morning tomorrow."

"Pretty happy?" said Trey. "I'm hoping for elated."

"She'll be excited to be back for sure, but she'll also be in pain from the surgery and a secondary issue that may leave her a little pissed at your friend Darell."

"What?" said Darell. "I thought I was a good guy here."

"No doubt she'll come to appreciate that after the discomfort subsides from the three ribs you broke doing CPR," Dr. Cole laughed.

"Whoops, it was well-intentioned."

"Normal collateral damage. She wouldn't be here without it."

"Dr. Cole?" asked Trey. "Can I spend the night with her?"

"I knew you'd want that, so I have a bed for you. You won't be with her until after we remove the intubation tube and begin the wake-up process, but you'll be the first thing she sees when she opens her eyes tomorrow."

Another bear hug and a few tears. "Thank you for everything," said Trey.

"I know you two have a newborn to check on today. Enjoy that and we'll see you again later. In a couple of hours, I'll be able to give you the full report on today's surgery, the overnight and morning plans, and get you settled in your bed for sweet dreams."

"Thanks again."

Trey entered Audrey's room first and immediately turned around, saying in a loud voice, "Sorry, I didn't know."

Audrey laughed out loud. "You've never seen a boob before?" She was breastfeeding Elizabeth.

"Usually not without an invitation," he laughed back.

"I covered up, come back."

Oohs and ahhs from Trey and Darell as they looked at the top of the tiny head poking out of the sheet that covered Audrey's chest.

"What do you think, Dad?" asked Darell of Richard.

"I think I've been gifted with the two most beautiful females on the planet."

"I believe Lincoln does too. He seemed pretty excited when he got the news."

Dr. Thibideaux knocked and entered.

"They never do sleep," said Darell laughing.

"Audrey," said the doctor. "I hear the feeding is going well."

"Anne had prepared me for the worst. She told me not to be disappointed if Elizabeth and I took a day or two to figure it out, but she took right to it, and it's been no problem. I think we're a perfect fit."

"Regina got a couple of hours of sleep after the delivery, but she already called me this morning. She was very pleased to hear Elizabeth could already take your milk. That's a big relief medically as far as nutrition and health."

"Dr. Thibideaux," said Richard. "Thanks for taking good care of my girls. It seems like things have gone remarkably well. Is it always this easy?"

Thibideaux laughed out loud. "Almost never, probably less than ten percent of deliveries and the transition to feeding go this smoothly. Someone is watching over you for sure. Elizabeth joined us early as a healthy complete infant no less prepared for the world than any full-term arrival. If I didn't know better, I'd say we had the dates wrong on the pregnancy count."

"It's Vicki," said Audrey. "Vicki is watching over us."

"She'll be back tomorrow," said Trey, misty-eyed again.

"Did you hear that, Elizabeth?" Audrey almost whispered to the tiny head. "Aunt Vicki will be so excited to meet you."

"They're reassembling her shortly, at noon," said Darell. "And Trey will spend the night to wake her up. Will you be coming home tonight?" he asked Richard. "Lincoln was asking about you."

"I think so. I'm told the best prescription for the next couple of days is some mother-daughter bonding time."

"Very true," offered Dr. Thibideaux. "Give them that time now. You get the rest of your life to enjoy them both."

Richard kissed his two girls on their foreheads. "See you lovely ladies tomorrow." He headed down to the ICU with Trey and Darell.

When Vicki's procedure was completed, Dr. Cole joined them in the waiting area.

"Well?" asked Trey tentatively.

The doctor said, "All the pieces fit just fine. No lingering edema concern, and all systems are go for a morning wake-up call. Medically, we consider this a relatively short-term coma. That means no real concern for any muscle atrophy or other short- or long-term negative conditions. In your terms, by tomorrow we can consider her in NFL concussion protocol and proceed accordingly. We can all rest easy tonight."

Turning to Richard, Dr. Cole put out his hand and said, "Congratulations, I hear your news is equally good."

"It is."

"Your gang is so efficient scheduling all of your hospital work at the same time," continued Dr. Cole, still laughing. "I hope you two have some celebratory plans for the evening," he said to Richard and Darell. "I'm keeping Trey here for the big reveal in the morning."

Hugs all around.

Lincoln was a wild beast when he saw Richard. It took almost forty minutes of frisbee time to knock him out.

HOSPITAL DAY FOUR

VICKI SQUEEZED TREY'S HAND AS SHE opened her eyes to see his smile. Her first word was "Ouch."

"Ouch?"

"Ouch."

"Do you know where we are?" asked Trey.

She squeezed his hand harder. With a big stretch and a shiver, she answered, "I know everything." Giggling. "Ouch, don't make me laugh."

He reluctantly removed his hand from her grasp. "I'm going to get Dr. Cole."

Dr. Cole was smiling when he entered the room. "Vicki," he said, taking her hand. "I'm Dr. Cole. I'm happy to meet you."

"Me too."

"We'll get to know each other better in the next day or so. I'd like you to do some simple things for me first. How hard can you grip my hand? Ouch," Dr. Cole this time. "Too hard. Very good. Can you raise your arms while I shine this light in your eyes?"

Arms raised, pupils perfectly reactive.

"How about moving your legs?"

Vicki kicked the bedsheets like an Olympic swimmer.

"Whoa," said the doctor. "We're still supposed to be in the slow stage. I see you're going to be a difficult patient now that you're awake." He chuckled, very pleased. "What is your pain level on a scale of one to ten?"

"Overall good but head pain a five or six and chest pain seven or eight."

"When you say chest pain, do you mean like a heart attack or like a muscle or bruise pain?"

"Muscle or bruise. Why do I have that?"

Dr. Cole laughed. "We'll get your friend Darell to explain that later. Trust me, it's normal and not a bad thing, but it will be painful for a couple of weeks. The pain we can take care of once we know everything else is good. Can you count backward for me, ten to one?"

With no hesitation, "Ten, nine, eight, seven, six, five, four, three, two, one, liftoff."

Can you tell me the months of the year in reverse from December?"

"December, November, October, September, August, July, June, April, no May, April, March, February, January."

"Do you think you can do a sit-up in bed?"

She started to, but the pain was overwhelming, and she gasped.

"My bad. Let me help a little," said Dr. Cole, moving some pillows and assisting her to an upright position.

"Let's see how your balance is if we try to sit on the edge of the bed. Trey, make sure that IV line is free. It should have plenty of length for what we need."

Vicki perched on the side of the bed while Dr. Cole did basic arm and leg reflex tests.

"Last task for now. Stand up by the bed. I'll hold you to make sure you're stable."

No problem.

"Can you do a squat?"

She did two, holding her arm against her ribs.

"Overachiever," said Trey laughing.

"Well, Vicki," said Dr. Cole, "Given your experiences of the past few days you're a remarkably healthy and blessed young woman. Let's get you back in bed. We'll do more cognitive tests and scans throughout the morning, but I'm confident they'll all go well. Trey, will you be staying with Vicki through the morning?"

"You couldn't keep me away."

"Good. As long as you'll be with her, I'm going to release her to begin eating as she feels up to it and allow her to get up for bathroom visits."

Vicki interrupted, "Any chance that includes a Waterpik and a toothbrush? I feel like I've been sucking on a dirty sock."

"We call that xerostomia and, yes, we can fix that. Trey, no walking outside of the room yet and keep her supported as needed. Vicki, you may find yourself very hungry in a bit but go light on your first meals, maybe some oatmeal and juice to begin. If you tolerate that well, you'll have no further restrictions on food. After we get the rest of your tests and scans, we'll remove the IV and you can start exploring the building. I know you have someone you'd like to visit."

"I can't wait to see Elizabeth again," she thought, nodding her head.

The rest of the tests went well, and Vicki tolerated food and drink with no issues. Dr. Cole even allowed her to shower with Trey in the room. After a rest in the early afternoon, they made a surprise visit to Audrey.

Before entering, Trey stood in the doorway and yelled, "No naked tits."

"Just a sec ... Okay, no naked tits."

He wheeled Vicki into the room where Audrey was breast-feeding Elizabeth.

Audrey was initially stunned as if witnessing a miracle. It took her a couple of seconds to speak, "Oh Vicki, are you okay?"

"Probably better than you, I didn't have to shit a football yesterday."

Half laughing, half crying, Audrey said to Trey, "Apparently she's back to normal."

"Oh yea, she's broken out of the witless protection program in the full Vicki persona we love and tolerate."

"In that case, nice turban," said Audrey.

"I wanted to make a good first impression on Elizabeth, I can't wait to hold her." Vicki stood up from the wheelchair and walked to the bedside.

"I'm in the hall if you need me," said Trey, closing his eyes when Audrey pulled the sheet down again, exposing her suckling breast. "You three can bond." He felt his way out.

"Meet Elizabeth," said Audrey, detaching the infant from her breast and handing her over to the smiling Vicki.

"We've actually already met."

"Really, how is that?"

"Audrey, I have so much to tell you about the adventure I've been on. You're probably the only person in the world that would believe me, maybe you and Abbey. We'll have to visit her too."

Still laughing/crying, Audrey said, "You're the only person I know that would call dying an adventure."

"It is the greatest adventure ever! You'll find out someday, hopefully, a long time from now. You have too much to live for with this little morsel," Vicki said, snuggling the baby. "Elizabeth, remember me from the Portal?"

"The Portal?"

"It's like a long vertical tunnel of light. We all pass through it when we're coming and going between here and there. That's where I've been. I wasn't dead and I wasn't living and I got to hang out with others who were both. I saw Clyde there." Clyde was Audrey's fiancé who was shot to death in a tragic accident just before they were to be married several years ago.

"You saw Clyde?"

"I did, he looks great in the Portal. I also met Richard's late wife and son, Gwen and Steven. Everyone in the Portal is healthy and perfect. They can't come all the way back, but they can come close enough to know how we are. Clyde and

Gwen and Steven are so happy for you and Richard and your lives together. They also met Elizabeth when I did, when she was on her way here."

"Vicki, you're right. Abbey and I may be the only ones who could hear this from you and not question it."

"I haven't even told Trey yet."

Audrey laughed, "You may need to give him a little time on that one. He's not an early adopter on the psycho abilities."

"You mean psychic?"

"That too." More laughter. "Vicki, I'm so glad you're back, and I'm so glad you're you!"

"We'll have lots of time to talk. Cover up your boobs so Trey can come back. We'll see if he's an early adopter on holding a baby."

He started out awkward and unsure, but Elizabeth took to him immediately.

"What do you think?" asked Vicki.

"She's so tiny."

"Everyone can't start at 6'7" like you did. I'm surprised your mom survived that delivery."

"Me too," said Trey, joining the laughter. "I guess that's why Dad always called her stretch."

HOMECOMING

VICKI AND AUDREY AND ELIZABETH ALL GOT released from the hospital on the same day one week after their life-changing events. Trey and Richard thought it would be a good idea to keep the girls together for a few days at Richard's house as a transition back to a new normal. With Darell's help, they had set up and decorated the great room as a ward of sorts for the homecoming.

"Wow," said Audrey as the guys introduced them to their temporary quarters. They were greeted by a giant "Welcome Home" banner at the entrance. Two queen beds had been moved in for Vicki and Audrey, and the newly refurbished crib was there. Elizabeth also had a new floor bed with bolsters strategically placed in a sunspot for daytime naps. Audrey's sketch pad and pencils were there, and Trey had gathered Vicki's essential crystals for her nightstand. Bright flowers and pink balloons were everywhere. Soft classical music played gently in the background.

"Will this do for now?" asked Richard.

"I love it!" gushed Audrey as she placed Elizabeth in the cradle and gave Richard a big hug.

"Nice job, guys," said Vicki with her arms around Darell and Trey. "If you have room service, we may never leave here."

"This will be your private space for as long as you need it," said Richard. He picked up two small hand bells and shook out their gentle rings. "These are for you. Your butlers will be on call for anything you need or desire."

"I love this floor bed for Elizabeth," said Audrey as she moved the new infant from the crib to the ground in a comfy wrap of soft blankets. "But we're still missing one family member for the real homecoming."

Lincoln had been impatiently waiting in the yard as he had watched the adults enter the house. Darell had been trying to distract him with the frisbee, but he was having none of that. His peeps were all here, and he raced in with barking zoomies as soon as Darell cracked the door, welcoming everyone with giant jumps and hugs all around.

"Let's all sit," said Richard. "And give him a minute to calm down."

And calm down he did, moving from petting hand to loving rubs among all his favorite people, missing no one ... until.

Lincoln noticed the little mattress in his favorite sunspot.

All were quiet as he tentatively wandered in Elizabeth's direction with sniffs and little sneezes, inspecting the new package. Lincoln gingerly stepped over the bolster to look at the latest arrival, no barking, no jumping, just quiet curiosity.

He walked slowly in little circles, trampling down the blankets on what he deemed to be his side of the bed. With a look at his collective parents, Lincoln laid down and stretched out with his back against Elizabeth, let out a little shudder and a contented sigh, and closed his eyes. Those two were bonded forever from that moment.

THAT FIRST NIGHT

WHILE THE MARRIED COUPLES MINGLED with the kids, Darell did the dinner honors, grilling some rib eyes, veggies for Vicki, and corn on the cob to go with a big Caesar salad and garlic bread. It was a very relaxed evening with beers and cigars for the boys. The grown-up ladies sipped champagne, and Elizabeth feasted on intermittent breaks of mother's milk. Everyone bedded down early, exhausted and comfortably content.

Vicki heard the tinkle of the hand bell first. She thought it was Audrey ringing for a butler, but Audrey was still fast asleep. The next noise was the *ping, ping, ping* of a basketball outside. Now she was fully awake, responding to the sound that had previously been a haunting premonition in the old house. The grandfather clock chimed 3:00 a.m. as she pulled on her robe and went to investigate.

Darell was alone in the driveway, shooting hoops under the floodlights.

Stepping out onto the porch, Vicki said, "I was expecting the ghost of Tom," referencing past occurrences.

"Not this time," said Darell. "Tom's happily ensconced at Ivy Hill Cemetery. Just a guy who couldn't sleep tonight over the snoring of Richard and Trey. I guess I woke you. Sorry."

"Actually, I woke up to the sound of a small bell before I heard you. Maybe a new message from the house's history." Richard and Audrey's house had been a source of much mystery dating back to its Civil War time. They were all well acquainted with its past sights and sounds. "I know the rest of you are skeptical of the paranormal world, but that's one of the things that draws me to this place. I love the surprise visitors."

"Well," said Darell, joining Vicki on the porch. "You made a converted believer out of me after living through all of last year's events."

"That's good," Vicki said smiling. "Because I have an update for you that you wouldn't believe otherwise."

"And what would that ominous message be?"

"I met Scott Marshall."

"Scott Marshall? The other dead high school kid?"

"Yes, he's still dead."

"I'm going to grab a bottle of water while I process that. Can I get you anything?"

"Water is good."

Darell churned up some memories on his way to the kitchen. Scott Marshall and Eli Dean were two recent high school graduates who were killed and buried on this property two years ago. Darell had turned up their names when he was investigating another death, Richard's first wife.

Darell handed Vicki a water as he pulled up a rocking chair next to hers and took a deep breath. "You have my full attention."

"Remember how we got cryptic messages and signs from the souls who had died here?"

"That would be hard to forget."

"But we never had any contact from Scott."

"I figured he was shy," laughed Darell.

"Maybe he was, but he did send us a sign after all. We just didn't know what it was."

"Okay?"

"It was the basketball. He never spoke to us, but we always heard the basketball before new events occurred. Scott Marshall played basketball at Wakefield High School."

"I did the police investigation, and I didn't turn up that detail. How would you know that?"

"Scott told me."

Darell took a big slug from his water bottle. "I knew I should have grabbed a beer."

"Probably, it's a long story, one I haven't told to anyone but Audrey, but I feel like I need to share it with everyone as they're ready to hear it."

"I think I'm ready. Am I ready?"

"I guess we'll find out." Long pause looking at each other. Vicki continued, "When I was in a coma, I stayed in a place that I call the Portal. It's like a tunnel of luminescence and fog that connects what we think is real with what is real, the source of where we come from and where we go to. We all passed through it on our way here, and we'll all pass through it on our way home."

"Yeah, I do need a beer."

Darell was gone for a little while, returning with two beers, having consumed half of one on the short walk back from the fridge, and another before that while he did some quick research on his phone. "Scott found you hanging out in the Portal and casually mentioned his basketball career?"

"Kind of. You don't really have conversations in the Portal, but you do exchange energy and thoughts. So, in that sense, yes. He told me that the basketball was his way of sending us a message."

Another long silence.

"Was Scott the only other person floating around with you?"

"Heavens no," said Vicki excitedly. "I met Elizabeth there on her way to Audrey and Richard. I also met Richard's deceased wife and son, and Audrey's former fiancé."

Darell opened his third beer. "How about the cast of 'Bubba Ho-Tep'? Any Elvis or JFK sightings?"

"Smart ass. I was afraid you wouldn't get it."

"Just trying to break my own ice. I checked the Wakefield yearbook on my phone, and Scott did play basketball there. You shouldn't have known that, but you picked it up somewhere in your travels. I think I want to believe your journey, just trying to absorb a little more alcohol to help me get there."

Yellow Cat strolled onto the porch and lay down between them. Yellow Cat was a feral occupant of the surrounding grounds, having shown up with other mysterious sightings in the history and mystery of the old house. The cat stretched out and commenced to lick its privates.

"Yellow Cat," said Darell. "Are you up on this tunnel of light between here and there where disembodied souls wander and share their wisdom?"

Eye contact, a loud meow, and a return to licking.

"Okay," said Darell, looking at Vicki. "I'm a believer. I know you were a dead woman. I promise I accept that you transcended something in your death, and I'm on board."

"Thank you."

Back into the quiet night with only the sound of crickets and a cat cleaning itself.

"I'll absorb more later," said Darell as he drained the last beer and headed to the door. "I'm going to try and catch a little more sleep. You probably should too."

"I will, I do need to thank you for one more thing."

"What's that?"

"Thank you for breaking my ribs."

"Anytime," Darell laughed.

After Darell went to bed, Vicki snuck into the upstairs bedroom and curled up alongside Trey. She had so much to tell him too.

MORNING HAS BROKEN

RICHARD, JOINED BY LINCOLN, HAD BEEN puttering in the kitchen for almost an hour. Coffee was made. Pancakes and Danish were staying warm in the oven, waiting for the guests. Lincoln hovered expectantly through the food prep and snapped to attention when Darell came in.

"Good morning, Dad," he said to Richard as he accepted his first cup of coffee. "How does that feel?"

"Life altering. I was just thinking it's been less than two years since I was alone in this big old house. Then I met you and Lincoln and Trey and Vicki and Audrey and now Elizabeth, and you're all here waiting for me to feed you."

"Glad we could enrich your lonely life, if only by making you a better breakfast chef."

Trey and Vicki were greeted by Lincoln as they joined the Coffee Klatch. "I slept like a log," announced Trey.

"More like a chainsaw cutting logs," said Darell. "I was up at 3:00 a.m. shooting hoops to escape you."

"See any ghosts out there?" asked Trey. Vicki, standing behind Trey, looked at Darell and put a finger over her lips.

"Just the usual suspects."

"I guess Elizabeth slept through the night, that's a good start," said Vicki. "I'm going to bring Audrey some coffee and check on the two of them."

Vicki left with Lincoln at her heels. "Do you guys have any plans for the coming days?" Richard asked. "I know we all have lives to return to, but I'd be happy to host everyone for a while as Audrey and I navigate our first baby days. I was also thinking we might all stay close to Vicki while she continues recovery."

"I'm with you," said Trey. "I think Vicki and Audrey could use some close time for at least a week to support each other. Us guys mean well, but I think they're their own best therapy."

"I agree," said Darell. "Especially when you add Elizabeth in the mix. I need to get back to the job thing, but I'll be checking in regularly, and I'll be here if anyone needs me for errands or company."

"Thanks, you two are lifesavers, literally," said Richard.

"Well at least Darell is," added Trey.

"Psshaw," said Darell. "It takes a village."

"Vicki and I will run by our place for a few hours to pick up some things and check on the shop," said Trey. "I know Michael and Michele have things covered there, but they're taking on some handyman projects, and I might be able to lend a hand throughout the week, so I'll see what's on the schedule. I also know they'd love to see Vicki in person after all the recent events."

"Sounds good," said Richard. "Secretly I'll be glad to get all of you the hell out of here for a couple of hours and have a little quality time with my wife and daughter. If you guys can set the table, I'll get started on the bacon and sausage."

Darell volunteered, "I got that covered, Trey can be the official taste tester for the meats."

"I do need my protein," laughed Trey.

Meanwhile, in the great room Audrey was feeding Elizabeth while a curious Lincoln watched. Vicki filled in Audrey on the night happenings with the bell and the basketball. "I'm not sure if the bell thing was a dream, but the ping ping ping of the basketball got me out of bed."

"Glad it was just Darell this time."

"I suppose, but I'm really feeling a calling to staying in touch with whatever is out there. It's more real to me now than it's ever been, and I hope I can hang on to that connection."

"I'm a little jealous that you got to meet Elizabeth before I did. You've always had that supernatural calling. Now it seems that it's calling back."

"I did get to share the Portal visit and the basketball connection with Darell."

"The basketball connection?"

"I guess I hadn't told you that one. Scott Marshall was another person I met in the Portal. He was the other teenager who was buried on the property here. He played basketball in high school, and that was his way of reaching out to us."

"Wow!"

"Wow for real. I know there's so much more to learn. I just need to figure out how to get back there."

"This might fall into the 'be careful what you ask for' realm. Remember that curiosity killed the cat. You had to die to get there. That's pretty high stakes."

"True," said Vicki pensively. "Still, I feel like there so many missing puzzle pieces there to complete important pictures."

"What do you think about a visit with Abbey? Elizabeth should be ready to travel in another month or so. We can call Abbey this week and start working on it."

"Sounds like fun. We can be Thelma and Louise, and Elizabeth can be Brad Pitt."

"I think I'd rather cast Darell for the Brad Pitt role. I'm sure he'd like to visit with Don while we're there. And maybe we could change the ending of the movie. I'm not as anxious as you to visit the Portal."

"Whatever you say, Thelma."

"Enough. My boobs hurt, I'm ravenous, and I smell bacon. Time for breakfast."

OFF TO THE PEACOCK PLUME

VICKI HEARD THE LITTLE BELL RINGING again when she walked through the door at the Peacock Plume and wondered why. Definitely not a dream this time. They didn't have a doorbell at the shop, so she knew it was a sound just for her.

"Namaste," she and Trey were greeted by Michele and Michael. "You look great!" said Michele.

"Thanks," said a smiling Vicki. "You do too, I didn't know when I'd get back here again."

As Vicki and Michele hugged, Vicki knew what the bell meant. She had a sudden and very clear vision of the aurora borealis pierced by the bright lights of the Imagine Peace Tower. She also sensed the name Bob. That's odd.

"Iceland," said Vicki.

"Iceland?"

"Iceland. Did you happen to be thinking of Iceland? I had an image of it when I hugged you. And do you know a Bob?"

Michele and Michael both looked at Vicki. "No way," said Michael. "Before you walked in, we were just talking about

Michele's dad, Bob. Iceland was one of his favorite places on Earth."

"Today would have been his birthday," added Michele.

Trey joined Michele and Michael, staring at Vicki. "How could you know that?" he asked.

"I'm not sure, but I did. As soon as we touched, I saw a picture of the Northern Lights and the Peace Tower in my mind, and the name Bob."

Contemplative silence against a soundscape of Kitaro's "Caravansary" instrumental softy emanating from the shop's speakers.

Michele spoke first. "Does that happen often?"

"Never," said Vicki. "Never before. I've always had senses of things like that since I was a little girl, but I've never seen such a clear message as just now."

"Are you okay?" Trey asked, putting a hand on Vicki's shoulder. "You look pale."

"I do suddenly feel a little drained."

"Let's go up to the apartment, and you can lie down for a bit."

Trey got Vicki upstairs and settled and returned to Michele and Michael.

"Is she okay?" asked Michael. "That was a little scary."

"I hope so. Everything has been a little scary lately. The doctors say all is well, but it's still so soon since I lost her. If you two are comfortable holding down the fort here, Vicki and I will stay at Richard and Audrey's for a week or so. I think giving her quiet time with Audrey is the best medicine for now."

"You don't have any worries here," chimed in Michele. "Business is good and we can handle everything here just fine, forever if you need."

"Thanks guys, I'm glad you're here."

"I've been doing prep work on the customer bathroom," offered Michael. "I think I can have it all ready so we can do the tile floor and wallpaper together on a Sunday when the store is closed."

"Can I help with that?"

"I don't think we'd survive the comedy of you and I trying to work together in that same small place," Michael laughed. "But I was thinking of painting an accent color on the wall beside the stairway. Maybe you could do that while Michele and I tackle the bathroom."

"I'm in," said Trey. "I'm going to run upstairs to check on Vicki and gather some stuff to take to Richard's."

RICHARD AND AUDREY

ELIZABETH WAS LYING ON A BLANKET IN her floor mattress, Lincoln nestled beside her. Between her gurgling and his little sneezes, it was obvious both were quite comfortable and content.

Audrey brought two cups of coffee and curled up against Richard on the big couch in front of the fireplace. "What do you think, Dad?"

"I think you're the second person to call me Dad this morning. I like it. I'll like it even more when Elizabeth says it."

"I wonder if she'll say Mom or Dad first."

"Pretty sure she'll say Lincoln first."

"Good point."

"This is nice," said Richard. "I think this is the first time our little family has been home alone. And who knew zoomie barky Lincoln would be such a natural babysitter."

"He's very intelligent and sensitive, just like his dad."

"That's sweet."

"I mean he knows how to stay out of the way and keep his mouth shut around the ladies."

"Nice."

"Maybe a genetic gift."

"On the topic of genetic gifts, that's a fine beautiful daughter you've delivered. Are you ready to get started on the next one?" he said suggestively.

A reflective silence as Audrey sipped her coffee.

"Too soon?" said Richard as Lincoln got up and nuzzled Audrey, tapping his feet in a little dance. "What's up with him?"

"I think that's the diaper dance. He did it last night too. It seems Lincoln has assigned himself to be the poop watch alert. Are you ready to try your first intervention there?"

"Absolutely, never let it be said that I am not the perfect husband and father when it comes to child raising." Richard scooped up Elizabeth along with her blanket and laid her on the coffee table. "Let's see how this works," he said as he fumbled to open the sticky strips on the diaper.

"Hoooooweeeee!" exclaimed Richard, gagging as he recoiled from the contents of Elizabeth's wrapper.

Audrey laughed out loud. "Something wrong?"

"I'll say," said a stunned Richard as he stepped away from the carnage to gather the wipes, the Desitin, and a new diaper. "When did you switch her to a raw sewage diet?" He was also laughing as he still choked on the stench of the putrid surprise. "Oh my God, Lincoln, get away from there," he said as the dog curiously expressed an interest in the task at hand.

"He's proud of his little sister's good work," said Audrey, scratching Lincoln's head.

"I wonder if we have to report this as a toxic waste spill?" mused Richard as he tended to the cleanup and wrapped up the remains. "Forget what I was saying, I'm not ready to get started on another one of these any time soon."

He disposed of the waste and deposited a fresh Elizabeth back on her mattress, where Lincoln joined her.

"You did good," said Audrey. "I'm very proud of you for stepping up to the plate."

"I just hope the next one is a bunt, I'm not sure I'm emotionally prepared to handle another grand slam anytime soon."

"Maybe you could teach Lincoln to change diapers. He seemed to be interested in the process."

"I don't think he's the guy for the job. He's pretty smart, but there are some things he just doesn't seem to have an aptitude for. Like the time I tried to teach him to mow the lawn. What a disaster that was. I will volunteer Trey and Darell to try one of these. That should be a hoot."

"You wouldn't do that."

"Watch me, with friends like that who needs enemas. I'll spare Vicki the horror for now. She's had enough trauma."

"She certainly has. Thanks for asking them to stay with us for a week or two on the pretense of helping with Elizabeth. Vicki's recovery is a miracle, but I'll feel better staying close for a while longer."

"You two, I mean you three, take all the time you need. Like Lincoln, I know how to stay out of the way and keep my mouth shut around the ladies."

"Richard, Vicki went somewhere when she died."

"You mean other than the hospital?"

"Yes, she had a real afterlife experience. She's told me things she couldn't have known unless it was real. And she wants to go back."

Richard tried to come up with something stupid and funny to say. He had nothing.

"Did she tell you about visiting the Peacock Plume while she was in the hospital?"

"No."

"Trey told Darell and me that Michele and Michael saw her and talked to her that day while we know she was in the hospital. We looked at the tapes from the shop, and she wasn't there. They were talking to something they saw, but she wasn't there to see."

"I'm not surprised," said Audrey. "I've always known Vicki to have a special and real connection to things supernatural and stopped questioning it years ago. I believe she really did cross the next line. I'm not sure if it's something to celebrate or fear, but I want to be with her while she figures it out."

"We all want the same for you and her. Is there anyone else that could shed some light on the situation? Some professional expert in such things?"

"I think our friend Abbey Foster could help. She and Vicki share something special in their depth of the supernatural. We're going to give her a call and plan a visit when Elizabeth is ready to travel."

"Road trips are always a good idea. Any excuse for Twizzlers."

VICKI AND TREY

TREY CLIMBED THE STEPS TO THE APART-ment above and found Vicki resting in the master bedroom. He thought back to the first time he was here. He spotted Vicki at an after-party for a DC event, and they were in lust at first sight. She was the hottest little vixen he had ever seen, and he was the mountain of a man she was ready to climb. It didn't take much small talk and flirting for her to casually mention she needed a ride home, and within the hour they were together in this very room.

Vicki ignited something he had never felt before. The physical attraction was intense, but there was an almost spiritual something about her like no other woman he had ever known. He could still see the rose quartz amulet she wore dancing on a chain, their sweat mingling as she rode above him. Every inch and every ounce of his manhood filled her as she filled him with the aura of her very soul, both realizing and surrendering to an other-worldly connection. He knew at that moment she was the one he was meant to be with forever.

Vicki was to become his muse, his soulmate, and the love of his life. He was off kilter seeing her looking so powerless as she did now, her scarred head shaved. Asleep under a heavy blanket on the giant bed, she was so tiny.

Trey knelt by the bed and watched her. She startled him as her eyes snapped open.

"It's not polite to stare."

"I'm staring at the only thing that matters in my life."

"What happened to football, cigars, and beer?"

"I'm serious now, Vicki. The second I knew you were gone, so was I, and nothing else mattered."

Reaching for his hand, she said, "I was always with you, and I always will be."

"Promise?"

"I promise. I know that for sure now."

"How do you know that?"

"I'll tell you, but first," she said, throwing off the blanket to reveal she was naked. "I'm going to get very cold if you don't get in here with me to warm me up."

"Are you sure?"

"Quite sure."

Trey got naked as well and laid down beside her as she melted into his chest, her tongue seductively running along his neck, his cheek, and up to his ear, where she whispered, "I really need this," and slowly initiated the dance that never failed to hypnotize him, with that rose quartz amulet on its chain between her breasts. Magic.

They lay there quietly, completely together again.

"Thanks for welcoming me back," Vicki said.

"Thanks for being back. I knew when you were gone, and I thought that was the end of everything."

"I have some great news for you. There is no end to everything. I was never really gone. I was just visiting another place where we've all been and all will be again."

"I want to believe in that, but you know it's hard for me to understand what I can't see."

"I know. I don't expect you to understand, but you've always humored me in my journey."

"I do believe in you, and I believe you have a gift that lets you touch things I'll never be able to explain. There are a lot of things I've seen and still can't understand, like how you knew about Michele's dad and how you came to her and Michael when I know you were somewhere else."

"When I died, I went to a place of complete serenity. I call it the Portal. It's the channel that souls pass through on their way to this reality and on their way back to the afterlife. I met others that were traveling both ways, including Elizabeth before she was born. I never made it all the way through the other end. Darell's quick work and the skill of the doctors prevented that, but I learned so much more about the other world beyond this one. I believe the answers to everything that can't be explained are there somewhere. I want to go back."

"I don't want you to die."

"Silly, I don't mean I want to die. I just want to be able to go back to see what else is there. It's so close. In twilight sleep, either falling off to sleep or in that semiconscious time before fully awakening. I can see the Portal, but I can't enter it. Sometimes I imagine blurred faces trying to connect with me, but I can't make out the shapes or hear anything that is not muffled beyond recognition. I really want to connect, and I believe they do too, but it just doesn't happen."

"I want you to have whatever you want. Can I help?"

"I don't know. Maybe just putting up with all my craziness."

"After what we've been through, I don't think anything is crazy anymore. I think you have a real relationship with something I'll never know anything about. I want you to have that, if you don't have to die again, of course," he said with a smile. "I'm so happy you're back with me, and I never want to lose you again. I want everything we are together to last forever."

"Me too," said Vicki with a wink. "In the spirit of getting back on the horse again I have another idea."

"I'm not sure I'm fully recovered from the last ride."

Vicki giggled and hit him with a pillow. "Not that, you horny bastard. I want you to take me water skiing."

DOWN TIME

PIZZA AND BEER MADE THE MENU FOR THE evening as everyone gathered together. Trey and Vicki got settled in for a longer stay with the things they had gathered at the shop.

"I don't see you guys needing me this week," said Darell. "I'll save up some personal time with a regular work schedule and let everyone else relax."

"We'll definitely need you next week," said Trey. "Vicki insists that she's going water skiing, and we'll never do that without you again."

"If she's ready, I'm ready, but I'd prefer we do it without the dramatic flair of our last outing."

"Amen," chimed in Richard.

"Are you sure that's a good idea?" asked Audrey, turning to Vicki.

"Oh yeah, no problem. I'm already feeling normal so it's time to be doing normal stuff. Trey did make me promise to wait it out one more week. I'll honor his husbandly concern for now, but the season won't last long, and I want to get wet as often as I can before it's over."

"Sounds like that decision is made and planned," said Richard. "You guys want to join me on the deck for a cigar before we call it an early evening?"

"Only if it comes with beer," said Trey. Richard gathered the smokes and liquid refreshments, and they headed out to a nice night under the stars.

"This doesn't suck," remarked Darell as he let the smoke roll out through his nostrils and surround his head.

"Trey," asked Richard, "Are you sure Vicki is ready to ski again so soon?"

"She was ready to go now. I fended her off for now just to be sure. I do want her to be able to do whatever she wants but we'll all have time around her this week, and we can push it off further if need be. In our day out to the shop today she was completely her old self, so I think all will be fine."

"Okay then," said Richard. "My plan was to let her and Audrey have maximum time together with Elizabeth this week. I think they're also going to call Abbey Foster and maybe even make plans for a trip up north to visit. I need to find something to do to stay out of the way."

"There's a painting project coming up at the Peacock Plume. If you're willing to be a Ben to my Tom Sawyer, I just might let you help," offered Trey.

"Golly, Tom, that sounds ever so swell! Are you sure?"

"I'm sure, Ben," said Trey with a wicked smile.

"Witching hour for me," announced Darell. "I'm hitting early shifts this week and I'll set up time off for our cruise next week."

"It's a date," said Trey with a wink. "I'm looking forward to unveiling our surprise on the water."

"What's the surprise?" asked Richard.

"For us to know and you to find out," said Darell. "You will be impressed." Darell moved on, and everyone else headed to bed.

The attic in the old house was Audrey's art studio. She was often up at dawn before anyone else was stirring and headed there for morning coffee as the space filled with the natural morning light. Lincoln usually joined her. He and Elizabeth were still making soft sleeping noises when she rose, so she let them stay with Vicki in the great room while she basked in the sunrise, sitting at her desk with a sketch book.

For the next half hour, Audrey's pencil danced across the page, adding lines and swirls, creating familiar images. It was Vicki and Elizabeth in a misty background, holding hands and looking at each other intently. They were beautiful together, full of happiness and peace, exuding love. Elizabeth was no longer an infant. She was a young girl dressed in a skirt and sweater as if she was just coming or going to school. The two figures mostly complete, the misty background began to fill with shadowy images of family and friends when Lincoln came dashing up the steps to break the creative process.

"Good morning, Lincoln," she greeted him as Vicki followed, coffee in one hand, Elizabeth cuddled under her other arm.

"Everyone sleep okay?" Audrey asked.

"Elizabeth and I were out like fairy tale princesses when Lincoln woke me."

"The poop dance?"

"Yes, one of the fairy tale princesses seemed to have eaten a poison apple. It passed impressively without causing her any harm. Lincoln walked me through the diaper detail."

"Oops, we were hoping to spare you that. Richard found his first encounter there to be especially traumatic."

"Our men find common colds traumatic, it's just poop, and she's really good at it. She's probably hungry now."

"I can fix that," said Audrey opening her robe and taking the baby.

"You've been busy," said Vicki checking out the drawing. "You always make me look good."

"Just another random sketch. I'm not sure where it was going, but I like the way the two of you came together."

"It is the way the two of us came together. Elizabeth was that age and looked exactly like that sketch when I met her in the Portal. I don't know how you saw that, but you did."

Audrey laughed, "Apparently your heightened psychic aura is effectively contagious. It must be your new power of thought control."

"Could be," mused Vicki. "I think I'll test it. Maybe I could control Trey's mind to start thinking about a new car for our road trip. Thelma and Louise had a '66 Thunderbird."

"Thelma and Louise weren't hauling an infant and all the related diaper bags, car seat, crib, and baby stuff."

"I do love the Sienna minivan."

MAN OVERBOARD

AFTER TALKING WITH DR. COLE, TREY WAS able to push Vicki back another three weeks on the skiing debut. Today was the day.

Darell was the first one at the marina. He popped in at the office of Jay O'Connor, the dockmaster. "Any chance I can get someone to back Trey's boat in at the dock?" he asked.

"Anything for Trey, how is Vicki doing?"

"That's why we're here. Vicki is doing so well she wants to go water skiing."

"The last time I saw her she was fighting for her life and now she wants to go water skiing. I would be surprised if it was anyone else, but she's an amazing scrapper."

"She does have great recovery skills. You'll never know anything happened to her when you see her. She's the same old Vicki."

"Rocking good news! I can't wait to give her a big hug." Jay abandoned the work on his desk to open the key cabinet. "I'll get the boat myself. Anything else you folks will need before setting sail?"

"I don't think so. The rest of the gang should be here in about half an hour. Trey and I are planning a surprise."

"I hope it's better than the last surprise you gave us," said Jay, laughing.

"I predict this one will be an inspiring moment we will all remember fondly. Actually, for you there will be two surprises today. You also get to meet the baby Elizabeth."

"Oh, that's right, I completely forgot there was a new addition smack in the middle of all the other excitement. Maybe I'll get to steal another hug there as well."

"No doubt. Mom and baby will both be happy to see you. I'll get the cooler from the car and meet you at the dock."

When the boat was backed in and tied off, Jay helped Darell load the big cooler. "They should be here any minute," said Darell. "I just want to set up a couple of things before that."

"If you need anything from me, I'll be back at the office."

"Thanks."

Darell unlocked the boat and put the keys in the ignition. He pulled out all the life vests and spread them around the seating areas before picking up one of the round life preservers and taking it to the front of the boat. He made sure all the floor areas were clear and jumped back onto the dock as the party arrived.

"Permission to board, sir?" yelled Richard.

"Aye aye, mate. Ready to load with precious cargo. That would be you, Elizabeth," responded Darell. Elizabeth was already swaddled in her full body flotation outfit, looking like an Eskimo.

Jay O'Connor had abandoned his work again to greet everyone. "You look marvelous," he told Vicki with a big hug. "Great to have you back."

"Great to be back," said Vicki. "I'm told you were instrumental in my return to the living."

"The real instrument was the AED. All I did was get it to the dock so the real heroes could do their work."

"Don't belittle the positive energy and hope you brought with it. I wouldn't be here without all the thoughts and prayers."

"And who is this?" Jay said, turning to wrap Audrey and the Eskimo in a joint hug.

"It's Elizabeth, say hi to our friend Jay," said Audrey.

"Welcome Elizabeth," said Jay. "And welcome back everyone else. I'll let you get to your excursion, but I'll be a whistle away if there's anything I can do."

"Thanks," said Trey. "I think we have everything we need. I appreciate you and your exceptional hospitality. You definitely run the finest full-service marina anywhere. I promise not to test the limits of that again today."

"Good enough. Enjoy the water."

The group boarded the boat. Darell went to the bow where he had placed the life preserver. "Trey, can you help me with the line up here?"

"Yes, sir."

The two men were standing on the front of the boat when Darell whispered, "Sure you're ready for this?"

Trey whispered back, "Let it fly."

And Darell did just that, making a mighty frisbee toss of the life preserver, sending it out about twenty yards into the center of the water. "Man overboard," he shouted as Trey dove in.

Time froze.

Vicki, Richard, and Audrey with the attached Elizabeth all looked to the bow to see Darell standing alone and no Trey. Jay O'Connor stopped on his way to the office and began running back towards the boat. Everyone knew that Trey couldn't swim.

Vicki screamed first, joined by everyone shouting exclamations of grave concern. "Darell, save him!"

"I've got this," said Darell. He stood calmly on the bow wearing a big smile, hand up in a stop gesture to everyone else. "Just watch."

And watch they did. Fifteen yards out in the water Trey was on the surface. The style was more of a hulking Jason Mamoa than a swift smooth Michael Phelps, but it was nonetheless a strong confident display of real swimming.

"Oh my God," said Vicki. "He's swimming!"

They all watched in awe as Trey made it to the life preserver and back, tossing it up to Darell. "I believe you dropped this," he said, treading water at the dock ladder.

"Come aboard, Captain, you've earned your water wings."

As Trey exited the water, Vicki ran to him and jumped, wrapping her arms and legs around him. "You scared the shit out of me," she whispered, crying.

"It's okay now, Vicki," he whispered back, as he untangled her and set her down on the dock in a hug. "I felt so hopeless when I couldn't help you, and neither one of us has to fear the water again."

She pulled back to look up at him. "How did you do it?"

"I had to. The first day I left you at the hospital I asked Darell if he could teach me to swim, and he did. I had to do it for you."

By now the rest of the gang had gathered on the dock, a smiling proud Darell and a still shaken Richard and Audrey. "I always knew you channeled Tarzan," said Richard. "But I never saw this Johnny Weissmuller side of you. I feel inadequate being the only non-swimmer left in the group."

"Then you're next," said Trey. "I can teach you. It's all about the breathing," he said, winking at Darell.

"Good idea," said Audrey. "Maybe Elizabeth can start with you. If we're all going to be boating, we should probably all be waterproof."

"It's never too early," chimed in Darell. "We can get her started in a few months when she outgrows her Michelin Man float suit."

Jay O'Connor had been standing, relieved that there was no new emergency. "I can put the boat back if the show is over."

"No way," said Vicki. "I'm skiing today."

"All aboard," shouted Trey.

The water was perfect. Vicki showed no fear jumping in and getting right up to slalom for a good half hour to reacquaint herself with the scene of the crime. Her ribs were screaming, but she didn't say a word. She was glad to be back. "I got the rope," said Darell as she climbed onto the swim platform. "These things can be surprisingly hazardous sometimes."

"No shit?" responded Vicki. "I wouldn't have guessed that." She deadpanned to Darell's grin.

Darell took a little practice next, and the two aquatic acrobats were satisfied. Elizabeth was clearly unfazed by her first boat trip, alternately sleeping and gurgling with no signs of seasickness.

Skiing over, and no other boats on the water, Trey let the boat drift in the middle of the Potomac channel, just enjoying the glorious day. He thought about David Douglass, found the number that Jay had collected for him, and made a phone call.

"Hello."

"David, it's Trey Roadcap."

"Mr. Roadcap, I didn't have any way to call you back. I wanted to apologize again, and I guess I owe you for taking care of my bill at the marina."

"You don't owe me a thing. Everything turned out fine. How did things go with your dad?"

"I told him what happened. He wasn't happy, but he came around when I told him I met you and you said she'd be okay. He's a huge Giants fan. So, your wife is really okay?"

"Good as new. We're out on the water now, and she just finished up skiing. Would you like to talk to her?"

"That would be great if she'd like to talk to me."

Vicki already knew the whole story and took the phone. "David?"

"Yes ma'am, Mrs. Roadcap."

She giggled, "Call me Vicki, I'm not that old."

"Okay Miss Vicki. I'm so sorry for all the trouble I caused. I feel so much better that you're better."

"Oh, I'm fine. In fact, because of you Trey learned to swim, so I have to thank you for that."

"He didn't know how to swim?"

"Go figure, the big athlete who's been boating his whole life was always scared of the water. I also met some new friends in my hospital time, and I thank you for that too. Our meeting on the river that day might have seemed like a bad thing, but I assure you it turned out to be a good thing. I'm perfectly well and glad to be back on the water."

"That's so good to hear. I was afraid I had ruined everything for you and Mr. Roadcap when I found out what I had done. It's so great that you would call me and let me know things are okay."

"Better than okay. You got Trey over his fear of the water."

Trey motioned to Vicki. "Before you hang up, get him to text me his address."

"David, Trey wants you to text him your address."

"Will do, I'm glad you're all better and skiing again. Thanks so much for calling to let me know. It's a big relief."

"Thank you too, it all turned out fine. Bye bye."

Vicki asked Trey, "Why did you need his address?"

"His Dad is a Giants fan. I'm going to send him a care package. People who root for the Giants in this town need all the support they can get."

"You really are a good guy," Vicki gave him a peck on the cheek. "And thanks for learning how to swim."

"I can save you from anything now." Maybe, thought the universe.

"Hail to the Redskins, or whatever we're supposed to call them these days," offered Richard.

The group celebrated Trey's watersports debut back at the Craft house.

"Here's to new surprises," Richard said, toasting the day's events.

"Given our history together," Darell spoke. "We may want to amend that. Here's to new happy surprises."

"Good point," responded Richard. "I should have learned over the last year or so to be careful what I wished for."

Trey asked, "Richard, are you still up for joining me at the Peacock Plume for a painting party?"

"Of course, what could possibly be more fun?"

"Count me out," said Darell. "I have an unscheduled emergency on whatever day that is."

CHECKING IN WITH OUR PA FRIENDS

THE FOLLOWING WEEK WHILE DARELL WAS back at work, Trey and Richard hung out with Michele and Michael at the Peacock Plume, and Audrey and Vicki made plans.

"Vicki! I'm so excited to see you alive and well and sort of in person," said Abbey Foster as the Zoom screens opened.

"I've missed you too," said Vicki. "I can't wait to see you in person for real. I have so much to tell you."

Don Weston's image joined the screen while he fumbled for the audio connection. "Ladies," he said. "Thanks for the invite. You are all a bright diversion in my day."

"Hi Don," said Audrey. "Elizabeth was asking about you, and we thought we'd give her a look."

"I knew I should have powdered my nose before I joined the call. Only one chance to make a great first impression. Does this uniform make me look fat?" Don laughed.

Vicki chimed in, laughing as well, "I'm not sure the uniform has anything to do with that."

"Ouch, you are definitely back to your old self."

"You know we love you, Don," responded Vicki. "That's why you're the centerpiece in our upcoming plans. How would you feel about hosting some guests for a Pennsylvania reunion trip next month?"

"Mi casa es su casa. I'd love to have some company. Will the three king bedrooms at my bed & breakfast be sufficient?'

"One for Audrey and I and Elizabeth, one for Abbey, and one for Darell will be perfect."

"Hmm, maybe I should reconsider. I didn't know you'd be bringing that rat bastard Darell along," Don said with a huge smile.

"He's our chauffeur so Audrey and I can play with Elizabeth the whole trip. Trey doesn't know it yet but he's thinking of buying me a nice new van for our drive."

A new screen opened up and Darell joined the group.

"Hello everyone, sorry I'm late. I thought I had my shift wrapped up when I got a 10-100 emergency call."

"Ooh," said Abbey. "Sounds like real police work. How did it go?"

"You don't want the details," Don uninterrupted. "10-100 is code for 'out using restroom.'"

"It went swimmingly," said a proud Darell.

"TMI," said Audrey. "Are you all ready to hear the big plan?"

"Anything to change the subject would be welcome," said Don.

"Okay here it is. Vicki and I and Elizabeth are itching for a change of scenery with some special friends. My doctor assured us Elizabeth will be ready for travel next month, and we'd like to come hang out. Vicki wants to share her new paranormal story with Abbey, and we're hoping to find a great spot for a Ouija séance like we did when we first met."

"That's easy," said Don. "How would you like to visit Stonehenge?"

"I'm not sure our vehicle will be equipped for ocean travel," said Darell.

"It's not the real thing, of course," continued Don. "It's a replica model on a property in the woods near here. The property owner was an artist known for his whimsical taste in expression. The land is now abandoned, but I have access to it. It's a crime scene from an investigation that took place the year before we all met."

"Sounds very promising," said Abbey. "The Churchville campus drama was all over the news here. I know what took place on the school grounds, but I'm not familiar with the rest of the story."

"I had actually promised Darell a visit to all the involved sites when we got interrupted by our Civil War excursion in Virginia last year. This one was the home of one of our professors who ended up committing suicide at that location. We also believe the school provost, Isabel Helms, was murdered there, but a body has never been found, and it's still officially a missing persons case."

"If that's not fertile ground for a séance, I don't know what is," said Vicki.

"Don, do you know how accurate the Stonehenge structure is?" Abbey asked.

"Our professor was a little OCD, so I suspect it has pretty good detail. Why do you ask?"

"Just for some pre-research. There's a 2008 map of all the Stonehenge blocks. If this structure is faithful to that, I could use it to lay out how we would set up when we visit the site."

"Does it matter since it's not the real thing?"

"To some degree, no. It's still a celestially grounded pattern, so it's like a pentagram. You don't have to have the original to tap into the power of the design. I'll go with the assumption that it has a fairly complete level of detail to the original and use the map to see how we could prepare the site further for the best possible results."

"While you're doing the Stonehenge plan," Vicki chimed in. "I'm going to get with Michele at the shop to make choices on crystal preparation for the site. I've got some immediate thoughts, but she's a great source in that area, and I'll see if she agrees with my choices or can add some better ones."

"Pardon my ignorance of the occult," said Darell. "What do crystals do?"

"Primarily," said Abbey. "They create a welcoming environment for spirits."

"Like 'we'll leave a light on'?"

"Kinda sorta."

"Nice."

"Then it's settled," said Don. "Pick your dates and we'll make it happen."

PEACOCK PLUMING

THE NEXT MONTH PASSED QUICKLY. VICKI and Trey had moved back to their apartment at the Peacock Plume, and Richard and Audrey were settled into family bliss with Lincoln and Elizabeth.

The girls got together daily at either the shop or the Craft house, playing with Elizabeth and Lincoln and making plans. Vicki and Michele were much in agreement on crystal choices for the Stonehenge encounter. They selected their best examples and packed them accordingly for the trip.

Richard and Trey had amassed the skills to start their own painting contractor business by now. They preferred to keep their amateur status, but you can never have too many skills or tools to do manly stuff.

"Richard and I are making a supply run," announced Trey one day at the shop. "Can we bring lunch back?"

"It's only 9:00," said Vicki.

"It might take a couple of hours. We're looking for a special paint edging tool we saw on YouTube, and we may need to make a few stops to find one."

"In that case, I could handle a Double Whopper with Cheese," offered Michael.

"Ditto," from Michele.

"I'll do a single and a small vanilla shake to share with Elizabeth," added Audrey.

"You know better," said the vegan Vicki.

"Got it," said Trey. "Four normal Double Whoppers with Cheese, one single Whopper, one vegan Impossible Whopper, no mayo, fries all around, small vanilla shake, and unless I hear otherwise you are all getting real Dr. Peppers."

"Make mine unsweet iced tea." Vicki again.

"Richard, you're in charge of the food. I can't damage my reputation by ordering non-meat and zero-sugar items."

"Understood," said Richard, taking notes.

"Vicki, I'm taking your car. My truck is low on gas, and I don't feel like running all the way to Costco. Do you need anything out of it?"

"Nope, there's nothing in it. It's not a man cave like your traveling storage unit."

Richard blew a kiss to Audrey and Elizabeth, and the mighty men went to hunting and gathering. They were gone three hours before returning with the food.

"Thank God you're here," greeted Michael. "I was just a meal away from death."

"They probably got held up at the mall," said Audrey. "You know how men can spend hours looking through all the greeting cards and the shoes there."

While they were eating, the amateur contractors, Trey and Richard, went over the punch list of Peacock Plume construction items with the group. "It looks like we still have one more whole wall to paint," said Trey. "Audrey wanted an accent color on the rear gallery area. We need to pull all the pictures to do that. We already have the paint for that wall left over from the stairwell. All the painted walls need the trim areas finished in white enamel. Tile work needs another final scrubbing, and we'll be ready to reinstall all the newly painted electrical finish plates."

"Did you remember I wanted to repaint and move the shelves in the library and crystal rooms?" asked Vicki.

"I did. We'll officially call that the Phase Two new project and add it to the parking lot job of resealing the asphalt and painting new lines for parking spaces. I've been looking at buying the striping tool for that. For now," Trey said gathering up the trash from lunch. "Michael and Richard can help me take down the artwork. Michele, you're on Elizabeth watch. I need Vicki and Audrey to bring in the stuff from the car."

"Isn't he bossy today?" remarked Vicki.

"I'd say organized and motivated," said Trey. "Lots to do. Did you ladies get the stuff out of the car yet? It's open and the keys are on the console."

"Sir, yes, sir," barked Audrey as she and Vicki headed out the door.

But Vicki's car was nowhere to be seen. In its place was a new Sienna Platinum van finished in sparkling Wind Chill Pearl.

"No way," said Audrey. "Did you know this was coming?"

Vicki turned and ran to the shop door, opening and yelling, "Come quick, someone stole my car."

"Shit," said Michael, running towards the door and into the parking lot.

"Go," said Michele. "I'll stay with the baby."

Richard and Trey looked at each other and laughed out loud.

Vicki squeezed past the exiting Michael to plant a big kiss on Trey. "How did you know that was exactly what I wanted?"

"I guess a little bird told me," said Trey, smiling and kissing her again.

They joined a confused Michael in the parking lot. "So, your car isn't stolen after all?"

"I don't think so," said Trey. "It just got bigger and shinier."

Vicki giggled. With a wink to Audrey she whispered, "I think the mind control thing works."

ROAD TRIP

DIAPER BAG, CHECK; CRIB AND MATTRESS, check; Binky, check. Water, check. Twizzlers, check. Ouija board and crystals, yellow rope, check. Big bag of Morton's salt, check.

The drive to York, Pennsylvania, was very comfy in the new van. Elizabeth, as always, was no problem at all. She cooed and smiled when she got attention and was happy to sleep when her adults were otherwise engaged, a perfect traveler on her first big excursion.

"Anyone need a rest stop?" the attentive Chauffeur Darell called out at every exit.

"Good right now," said Audrey as she was breastfeeding Elizabeth. "But when we're done with breakfast, we usually follow up with a poop. Probably a half hour or so we'll want to take a break to make a change and destroy the evidence, so it doesn't mess with Vicki's new-car smell."

"Got it, that will work out perfectly for us to arrive at the Weston mansion all fresh and ready for a big lunch."

"Abbey texted me," said Vicki. "She's already there and waiting."

An hour later, they pulled into the driveway, Thelma and Louise and Darell and a freshly baby powdered Elizabeth.

"Welcome back," greeted Don from where he and Abbey were sitting on the big wraparound porch. "We'll help you unload."

The table was already set with a great spread of local cold cuts as they passed by on their way to the bedrooms.

"Nice," said Vicki. "I see some salad and veggies and hummus in the mix."

"I wouldn't forget you," said Don. "And I knew the sweet bologna, farmer's cheese, and Zerbe's chips weren't on your menu. I checked to make sure you could also enjoy the oatmeal cookies."

Rooms set up and lunch packed away, Don grabbed a couple of cigars for him and Darell and circled the rockers on the porch.

"Would Aunt Abbey like to do some Elizabeth bonding?" asked Audrey.

"You know it," she said, taking the bundle of baby.

"I'm so happy to be here," gushed an emotional Vicki with tears in her eyes. "Thank you for the hospitality, Don. You and Abbey are the best friends I couldn't wait to see again."

"Thanks for that," said Don. "We're glad you're back. Always a pleasure to see you and Audrey and a special pleasure to meet Elizabeth. But did you have to bring Darell along?"

"Hey, hey, I'm sitting right here."

"Sorry, I thought you were on 10-100 emergency again."

"This is the sweetest baby ever," Abbey spoke.

"Oh, you haven't met her at diaper time," laughed Darell.

"Stop," said Vicki. "She is the sweetest baby ever at all times."

"Vicki should know," said Audrey. "She met her before any of us."

"Really?" quizzed Abbey.

"Really," said Vicki. "I met her in the Portal when I was in a coma."

"Do tell?"

"Abbey, it was amazing. It's that place between here and there that we all pass through coming and going. It's real, and I can't wait to see it again."

"I think I really believe she was there," said Audrey.

"Well, I do," said Abbey. "There's a lot of academic research on near-death experiences and visions. You don't get much nearer than actually dying and staying in a coma for days. I even read a journal article recently suggesting that ketamine could produce a similar effect of the out-of-body state reported by survivors of those experiences."

"Sounds like we've transcended to another level in the unknown," said Don. "I have to admit I'm still a partial skeptic in the workings of the netherworld, but you ladies make me want to believe more all the time."

"Believe it," said Darell. "Vicki came back with some details about last year's investigation that I didn't know, and she couldn't have known without some divine intervention."

"Interesting. I think it would take divine intervention to provide the final answer on my missing person mystery."

"I guess we'll find out tomorrow," said Abbey.

THE HUNDRED-ACRE WOODS

IT WAS ALWAYS AN ADVENTURE NAVIGATING the long unpaved, rutted path to the house in the woods. "I was up here six months ago," said Don. "I brought a chainsaw and cut back some of the bigger saplings and other brush that had accumulated on the driveway and around the house. The scene is exactly as it was left after the investigation over a year and a half ago, with the exception of Mother Nature's reclamation efforts."

Don parked by the remains of the old barn, a pile of burnt timber and ash. The charred piles of scrap, tools, unfinished welding projects, a large wood stove, and a number of pottery kilns dotted the large dark stain on the earth. "You can still see a bit of the cleared area where our teacher's body was found," said Don. "Middle-aged white male, classic pugilist position of a burning death. Autopsy confirmed asphyxiation from smoke inhalation, presumed suicide based on other evidence.

"There are two other areas of interest here. The A-frame house was the location of the deceased's laptop and suicide note. It also has a partially attached greenhouse that was used primarily for cannabis cultivation. Beyond the tree line in front of us is a large clearing. Let's walk up there first. I think you'll find the ideal spot for your Ouija séance."

As the group rounded the stand of trees, an open acre emerged. A quarter-scale model of Stonehenge with six-foot pillars surrounded the center of the clearing.

"Not quite to full scale. But more impressive than the 'Spinal Tap' version," said Abbey. "Definitely our séance site."

Vicki heard the now familiar tinkling of a bell. "This is the spot," she said. "Whoever wants to meet us is here and calling."

Audrey set Elizabeth, still in her car seat, in the middle of the scene. While the three women wandered the area, Don and Darell retrieved and set up the materials for a paranormal journey, chairs, a small table, and a bag with the Ouija board and the pouches of crystals.

"All good?" Don asked.

"Perfect," said Abbey. "Won't you be joining us?"

"Don't think so. I owe Darell a crime scene tour of the house and barn area. I think your collective energy is better suited to the task at hand without any influence from us."

They left the ladies to their preparation, and Don took Darell in through the greenhouse, adjacent to the A-frame's kitchen entrance.

"Nice setup for an herb afficionado," remarked Darell, inspecting one of the remaining survivor plants. "Good sun, irrigation, auxiliary grow lights, should have been ideal for a healthy personal harvest."

"You'll appreciate the pantry storage," said Don, walking him through the kitchen to open a heavy rustic door on the other end. Don shined a flashlight into the cavern, exposing canning jars full of sinsemilla buds.

"Any possible drug connections to your murders?" asked Darell.

"No, just a lifestyle choice for our suicide, Glenn Weaver. He was actually a very likeable, mellow guy."

"Let me guess," said Darell smiling. "Lived alone, sort of a loner, smart and quirky, few real social connections, our basic serial killer profile."

"I'd known the guy for a few years, and I never saw it coming," said Don. "I can't remember if I told you before, but there were some extenuating circumstances. In the month before the school fired him, he had received a terminal cancer diagnosis."

"Two big strikes. You shared those with me before."

"And the autopsy showed a brain tumor on the amygdala, same as Charles Whitman. Remember that one?"

"The Texas tower shooter?"

"That's the one."

"I hadn't heard that part."

"The medical examiner had a personal connection to that case and was quite intrigued by the finding in this one. There's quite a documented history since Whitman of other reasonable normal subjects surprisingly committing some totally out of character acts of gruesome violence."

"That is intriguing. Do you think that's what happened with your guy?"

"There wouldn't be any way to prove it, but it does fit the pattern."

"Anything else we should look at in the house?"

"I don't think so. Let's go check on the supernatural scene, and I'll walk you through the remains of the barn."

STONED HENGE

DARELL AND DON FOUND THE LADIES HAD been quite productive among the faux stones in the abandoned cannabis field.

"I wondered what the rope was for," said Darell, seeing it now laid out in a triangle shape among the stones, with the flat end going across the middle of the structure. That's where the table and chairs were set up. The Ouija board and planchette were on the table, along with a large print.

"Abbey used this map of the real Stonehenge to lay that out," said Audrey, referring to the chart on the table.

"You were right, Don, in suggesting that our deceased artist would be OCD faithful to the original," added Abbey. "This is a copy of a 2008 rendering by Anthony Johnson that is the definitive Stonehenge blueprint. All the markers are identified and numbered, and Glenn Weaver has faithfully recreated them here. We followed the replicas of the low fallen Bluestones 25 and 28 and Sarsen Stone Number 16 to triangulate with a base crossing the center spot of the monument where we placed the Ouija table."

Audrey added, "Vicki put together small leather bags of crystals that are placed on those three stones."

"Michele at the Peacock Plume helped me make the selection," said Vicki. "There are three crystals in each bag. Kyanite is there to stimulate the psychic environment and help in connections with our spirit guides. Rhodonite releases negativity and fear, allowing reassurance and forgiveness. Rose quartz is nurturing in unconditional love."

"But why the triangle?" asked Darell.

"It enhances the power of the space as a complement to the celestial arrangement of the stones," responded Abbey. "In its broadest sense it allows for an attraction of spiritualism and enlightenment. The base of the shape is also a symbol of protection."

"Protection from ...?" Don trailed off.

"Any potentially undesirable spirits that might try to join us."

"Is that a common problem?"

"I've fortunately never had an issue with it. How about you, Vicki?"

"Nor I, but in addition to folklore, there are a number of documented cases of séance and Ouija experiences that are attributed to uninvited guests from beyond. It doesn't hurt to respect that and allow for some caution in the design of the space."

"Why didn't we add the triangle when we did the Ouija stuff at the house?" asked Audrey.

"We didn't have Elizabeth with us," said Vicki.

"That," added Abbey. "And the Stonehenge environment, even though it's not the real thing, is an unknown influence. That's why we're also spreading a circle of salt around our Ouija séance setting as a protection circle against negative energies. I'm confident we have no fears with the extra preparation."

"Aren't the negative energies what you're looking for?" asked Don.

"We never know what will come to us," continued Abbey. "But the most likely visitors would be your missing provost and Glenn Weaver. It's presumed that they both suffered negative experiences that ended their lives at this site. That doesn't mean Isabel and Glenn have negative energies. What we're looking for is to offer them a channel for release of guilt or shame for those twisted endings, a chance to share the positive energy of their lives over the circumstances of their deaths."

Scratching his head, Don said, "I must say you ladies fascinate me with your abilities to make these connections. I've walked a lot of battlefields and don't doubt the presence of some sense of the anguished spirits that died alone in the grass and mud of that acreage. I've never been able to shake that feeling, but I always wrote it off as my imagination of the historical moments, until last year. When we did the archeological dig at the Craft home, the Ouija séance that you and Vicki and Audrey did surfaced some links in the physical and diary evidence that was irrefutable and couldn't have been confirmed in any other way. You made a believer out of me."

"Me too," said Darell. "By the way, I love this sketch," looking at Audrey's pad on the table. It was a long view of the cannabis field and the stones with the overgrown A-frame of the house in the background. In the middle was an outsized smiling Elizabeth on her floor mattress, giving the impression that the structures around her were playthings, like a mobile in a cradle. "I like the detail in the trees and grass."

"Thanks," said Audrey. "I'm not sure if it's done. I may add Lincoln as her constant companion and protector."

"It looks like you're all set to begin, so carry on, ladies," said Don. "Darell and I are going to peruse the remains of the barn. The forensic folks from the state covered every square inch, but we still have an open missing person case, and it never hurts to put fresh eyes on a crime scene."

"Happy hunting," offered Darell as he and Don moved on to the barn. He added, smiling, "May the force be with you."

CUV

VICKI WALKED OFF THE TRIANGLE ONE LAST time as Abbey spread the salt ring around the table. Elizabeth was sleeping in her car seat. Abbey moved the car seat to the edge of the circle, and the three women settled into their chairs to see what, if anything, would come to join them.

Vicki was to be the driver with Abbey as co-pilot. They were both heavily invested believers in the ritual they were about to embark on. Audrey was a believer in the paranormal senses she had witnessed in Vicki and Abbey but didn't feel the same depth of calling to a total commitment of the other world connections. She wasn't a total skeptic, having experienced unexplainable findings, but she still maintained a mental neutrality in looking for the explainable first. It was a good balance. Elizabeth, for her part, was sound asleep, lightly snoring.

The three adults at the table joined hands as Vicki began with, "We gather here to welcome friendly spirits that have been joined to this place. We reject negative forces that may attempt to attach themselves to our quest, looking only to offer an outlet of release for those that left us in troubled times. We welcome all that come in peace to connect with us and unburden your souls with your truths."

All hands moved to the planchette, and so it began ...

"My name is Vicki. Is there anyone here that would like to talk?"

Nothing for about twenty seconds. The planchette began to move, circling slowly and settling on YES.

"We have heard of two spirits that have been linked to this space by untimely death. One male and one female. Is that true?"

YES from the board.

"Are there any others that died here or wish to speak with us?"

NO

"Are you both with us now?"

NO. And a further slow move to the number "1"

"Are you male or female? You can answer by 1 or 2."

2

"Are you Isabel Helms?"

YES

"I'm happy to meet you, Isabel. My friends Abbey and Audrey and Elizabeth are also here."

In its abbreviated spelling the board communicated, I SAW U B 4

Pause.

Only Vicki could hear the growing tinkling of the bell in her head as the women exchanged quizzical glances. *Could it be?* Her mind raced through possibilities. "In the Portal?"

The planchette moved to YES.

Abbey and Vicki locked eyes at the revelation. Audrey's thoughts were on Elizabeth, the other Portal traveler.

Vicki spoke, "Were you the naked woman in the mist who followed me there?"

YES

The short silence was broken by a loud sound from the edge of the circle. It was something between a laugh and a cry that came from Elizabeth.

Ouija quickly spelled out, I MET U 2.

Audrey was nervous now and asked out loud, "Do you mean harm to my daughter?"

"NO ... HELP."

"Help for Elizabeth?" Abbey joined in.

YES

"Is she in danger?" asked Vicki.

MAYBE. The movement on the board continued, NOT NOW. SOON.

"Can you really help us?" asked Audrey, no skepticism now in her fear.

YES, and then CUV and GOODBYE

A strange noise almost sounding like "V" came loudly from where Elizabeth lay in her car seat.

New questions got no more response from the board.

"That's it for now," pronounced Abbey.

"It can't be," said Audrey in a raised voice, tears in her eyes. "We need to know more."

"We need to have faith that more will come in its time." Abbey continued. "Isabel means no harm and only wishes to help. I believe that. More will come in time."

"I don't like it," said Audrey quietly.

"I don't either, but I accept it."

"Me too," said Vicki reaching to hold Audrey's hand. "I know I'll see Isabel again. I don't know how, but I will. Trust me."

"I do trust you Vicki, but this is Elizabeth."

"Who I love as much as you do and promise to protect. I'll find Isabel again somehow."

Don and Darell were just returning from the barn. "Nothing new from our crime scene, just pottery kilns, old stacks of metal, the big wood stove, and lots of ashes," said Don. "How did your group make out?"

"Uh oh," said Darell, looking at the fallen faces and Audrey's tear-stained cheeks. "This looks serious."

"It is," said Audrey. "We met Isabel, and she said Elizabeth is in danger."

"Isabel?" asked Don Weston. "Isabel Helms?"

"Yes," said Abbey. "We know she did die here, and she left us a warning about Elizabeth, but it seems like she'll see Vicki again soon."

"Do you know how she died?"

"No, but it happened on this property. Our real concern is now the baby."

"That's now our concern too," said Darell. "What can we do?"

"Nothing until I find out more," said Vicki.

"How?"

"I don't know, but it will come. I know that."

"I'm sorry," said Don. "Maybe this was a bad idea coming here."

"Not at all," said Abbey. "We have more questions than answers, but that's not unusual for a first contact. Now we focus on what comes next. It was a good connection, and we need to be patient for more revelation to come. The site is dormant for now, so maybe it's time to pack up and move on."

The now somber group started folding chairs and breaking camp. Vicki went to gather the bags of crystals while Don walked off the yellow rope, coiling it as he went. Darell moved to gather Elizabeth and stopped before he picked her up. "Did anyone notice that the top of the car seat and Elizabeth's head were outside the salt circle? Is that a problem?"

"Abbey!" Audrey yelled. "You placed her there. Did you do that on purpose as some kind of experiment?"

"Audrey, I wouldn't do that. I thought she was in the circle."

"Does this mean she's infected by some sort of evil spirit?"

"No, no, no. We only met Isabel. And everything should have been safe with the triangle and its base where we set it up. The salt was just extra insurance."

"Should have been safe? But the sounds Elizabeth made. How can you be sure nothing touched her?"

"Honestly, Audrey, I can't be sure, but it could only have been Isabel, and she wanted to help."

"I don't like that Isabel said she met her before. How would you feel if it was your child at risk?"

"I'm truly sorry, Audrey. You're right. I made a mistake."

"A mistake that left my baby unprotected."

"Audrey," said Vicki as she returned to give her a hug. Audrey pulled away. "Audrey, don't be afraid. I promise you

I'd feel it if Elizabeth had been possessed by any spirit other than you and I. I promise she's fine. And I promise I'll find a way to get the answers we need from Isabel. I promise. Can you trust me?"

"Oh Vicki, I want to."

"But you're still scared, I know."

"I am."

"That's fair, but please, for me, accept that I will keep Elizabeth safe always."

"Audrey," said Darell as he picked up the sketch she had made earlier. "I see you added Lincoln 'the constant companion and protector' to the artwork."

"I didn't," said Audrey, looking at the picture.

"Well, someone did, and it sure looks like your work."

Softly, "It does."

Don, Abbey, and Vicki drew closer as everyone looked at the sketch in silence.

"I think it was Isabel," said Vicki. "Letting us know Elizabeth is already protected."

"As soon as we get back to Don's house, I'm taking my baby home."

That was the last word as the group finished packing and left Glenn Weaver's hundred-acre woods.

QUIET TIME

ABBEY WAS CRUSHED THAT SHE HAD HURT Audrey. She tried to make amends, but Audrey wouldn't even talk to her. Vicki did her best to console both separately as they got things packed and headed south. Darell snuck off to call Richard and Trey to let them know the group would be back this evening. He also gave them a little heads-up on the current happenings and moods.

The two-hour drive seemed like it was forever. All was good with Elizabeth as she alternated between happy baby noises and sound sleep. She ravenously assaulted Audrey's breasts, setting up a rest stop halfway to clear her evacuation of a big meal. Vicki and Darell tried to keep up encouraging small talk along the way, but Audrey remained silent. They got back to Arlington in record time.

A cheery "Welcome home, weary travelers" from Richard greeted them in the driveway. Lincoln jumped and barked, no doubt the same message. "We didn't expect you until tomorrow, but Lincoln and I already made our famous spaghetti sauce today, so we're ready for you. Trey is in the kitchen working on the garlic bread and salad. How are my girls?" he said, as he leaned into the van to collect Elizabeth in her car seat.

Audrey was feeling guilty about shutting out Vicki and Darell and Abbey. Elizabeth was obviously fine and normal. Audrey mustered up a smile for Richard, saying, "Plenty to talk about, but spaghetti sounds yummy."

Vicki perked up eagerly at Audrey's sudden animation. "You did make a vegetarian pot for me, didn't you?"

"Lincoln would never let me forget that. He handled and taste tested your sauce himself," Richard said, smiling.

Trey walked out of the house, handed Darell a beer, and almost got tackled by Vicki's leaping hug as she jumped high to wrap her arms and legs around him. "Miss me?"

"You know it."

"I'll make it up to you."

"Oh yes you will," Trey said, planting a big kiss as he carried Vicki up the porch steps. "Oh yes you will."

Darell filled the dinner talk with a Don Weston update and his crime scene wanderings, intentionally blocking out the Stonehenge encounter for now, closing with, "And I stole all Don's oatmeal cookies for our dessert."

That was the signal to clear the table and move to the deck, where an unusually warm autumn night was supplemented by a couple of gas space heaters, creating a cozy atmosphere for after-dinner libations and cigars.

"Did you just give Lincoln some oatmeal cookie?" asked Audrey of Darell.

"Maybe."

"Whoops," said Vicki. "Me too."

"Guilty," said Trey.

"Richard?" questioned Audrey.

"Just a little. Not a whole one."

"No more cookies," said Audrey, as she banished the tray to the out-of-reach deck railing.

Lincoln knew it was time to wander off in the yard for a bit. He had a belly full of cookies to take care of.

"So how is Abbey, and how cool was Stonehenge?" Richard asked, not letting on that Darell had shared some of the story.

"Abbey is good," piped up Vicki. "And Stonehenge was very cool. It was smaller than life size, but Abbey had a map of the real thing, and it was an exact stone-by-stone replica."

"A perfect setting for a Ouija séance," added Darell.

"Any new ghosts or goblins?" asked Trey.

"We met Don's missing provost, Isabel Helms," offered Vicki. "It turns out I met her before, back when I met Elizabeth for the first time. She knew Elizabeth too!"

"Really?" Richard said reaching down to pat Elizabeth. She was lying in the floor mattress at his side, now joined by Lincoln as he completed his wanderings. "Did you remember her, Elizabeth?"

"I think she did," said Audrey quietly.

Vicki broke an awkward silence. "Things got a little serious. Isabel warned us that Elizabeth may be in some danger."

More silence.

Richard this time, "A year ago I might have attempted some witty pun, but today I sit here with some permanent scars from our last Ouija warning."

"Isabel said she'd see me again," said Vicki. "I need to go back to the Portal."

"Not on my watch," said Trey seriously. "I don't ever want to lose you again."

"I agree," said Richard. "Isn't there another way to contact her? Another séance? Audrey? Darell? What are your thoughts"?

"I'm scared," said Audrey, tears in her eyes. "But Vicki promises it will work out, and I have to believe her."

"I've got nothing," said Darell. "I want to believe her too."

A strange noise almost sounding like "V" came loudly from where Elizabeth lay.

"I think Elizabeth is telling us she believes in Vicki too," said Audrey.

Lincoln barked once, sharply, and settled tight against Elizabeth.

"Then I guess we can only trust the process, whatever that is," said Richard.

PAIN

IT HAD BEEN A COUPLE OF WEEKS SINCE the Pennsylvania trip, and the Roadcaps were settled back into the routine of things at the Peacock Plume. Vicki's night was restless with some odd dreams and what started as a dull ache in the center of her belly and spread to her right lower abdomen.

"Sleep in, sweetie," she said, as she gave Trey a kiss. "I'm going down to visit with Michele and Michael."

The Millers were always in to start the day quite early. They really ran the shop on their own these days. Mornings before opening was their time to go over the previous day's receipts, prepare the bank deposit, and review any inventory orders.

"Good morning," Vicki greeted them as she came down the stairs from the apartment. "Good morning," they responded in unison.

"I was just getting ready to update the website and social media that you're back in residence," said Michele. "The regulars always miss you. Any special notes you'd like me to add?"

Vicki wanted to announce that she believed an alien was about to explode out of her abdomen but went with "How about a post-solstice crystal sale?" instead.

"Done, any special plans for the day?'

"*I hope not*," thought Vicki. She had been uncomfortable for many hours but didn't want to mention it and alarm anyone. She felt like they all saw her as fragile since the accident and likely would overreact.

"I'm going to steal a spot of tea and piddle with some of the displays. Is there anything in particular you think could use some attention?"

"Maybe just the crystal room for some placement and signage for a sale. I'm going to work on my jewelry cabinet when we're done with the business stuff. We should probably also apply the sale to the ones with appropriate stones in there."

"Alrighty then, yell if I can help with anything." Vicki hoped she sounded cheerful as she took her tea and turned away. She was almost ready to break as the pain became extra sharp and seemingly relentless, but it suddenly seemed to subside and dropped to a manageable level. "*Glad I didn't bring it up*," she thought, not knowing that her appendix had just burst and her body was already filling with poison from the wound.

Another hour passed. Vicki was rearranging some displays when she felt something really wrong. She was extremely hot and started sweating profusely. Waves of nausea hit her, and she yelled for Michele as she crawled to the trash bucket in the room and began vomiting violently.

"Oh my God, Vicki," Michele said, finding her on the floor in the crystal room. "Michael," Michele shouted. "Get Trey!"

Michele hugged a depleted Vicki as she heard the two men on the steps.

Trey was still in his boxers as Michele moved aside. Vicki looked up at him and whispered, "I think I'm really sick."

Trey didn't hesitate. "I'm getting dressed and we're going to the hospital," he told her. "Michael, call 911," he said, racing back upstairs.

Trey quickly pulled on some sweats. He could hear a siren as he returned to Vicki's side. "Hang on, baby, they're almost here."

Michael met the EMTs at the door and took them to Vicki, where they quickly set up monitoring for vitals and established communication with the ER. Fading in and out from pain and shock, Vicki was able to share enough of her symptom progression for the medical team to decide she was going straight to the ICU.

Dr. Cole met Trey at the hospital loading dock when the ambulance pulled in. "I'd like to say I'm happy to see you again," he said. "But under the circumstances, the pleasantries can wait. We're pretty sure Vicki's appendix has ruptured, and the OR staff is waiting."

"I'm glad you're here," said Trey. "I know she's in the best hands with you."

"Don't worry, we've done this before. Get settled and I'll keep you informed as things progress." Dr. Cole and the EMT's disappeared down the hall with Vicki.

Trey sat down in the familiar waiting room and called Audrey's cell phone.

"Trey," she answered. "To what do I owe the pleasure of your early morning call?"

"I'm at the hospital with Dr. Cole. They think Vicki's appendix burst, and they've taken her in for surgery."

"Oh no!"

"Oh yes. I guess it's serious, but Dr. Cole says not to worry."

"Then we won't worry, but we will be there soon."

"You don't need to do that. I think we'll be okay."

"I know you will, but we're on our way anyhow."

"I knew you'd say that. Michele is already on her way to your place to look after Elizabeth and Lincoln. She insisted, and I couldn't stop her."

"Good. Have you called Darell?"

"Not yet."

"I'll do that now and we'll see you soon."

"Thanks, Audrey."

While Audrey was calling Darell, Vicki was being prepped for surgery. The pain was bearable now, but she still found it hard to concentrate on the activity surrounding her. The

IV line was in, and the anesthesiologist told her to relax and expect a warm feeling. Vicki focused on a sink in the operating room and watched it slowly fade away as the propofol drip found its way into her veins.

Vicki was back in the Portal.

WAITING IS THE HARDEST PART

DARELL COULDN'T GET AWAY BUT PROM-
ised love and prayers. Richard and Audrey arrived at the
hospital while Vicki was still in pre-op. Trey was quiet but
surprisingly calm. "Dr. Cole is our lead guy again, so I feel
confident all will go as well as possible," he said.

"It was her appendix?" asked Audrey.

"They think so. They are treating it as ruptured. If it's not,
it will be a simple operation. If it is, apparently there are a lot
of things to worry about."

They talked about old times and little of consequence while
they waited. "Have you been practicing your breathing exer-
cise?" asked Trey of Richard. As a recent aquatic aficionado,
Trey was now teaching Richard to swim.

"Of course, maybe," answered Richard with a feigned hurt
look followed by a nervous laugh.

"I'm serious," said Trey. "You're in the deep end on our next
outing, so you better have that part down."

"Yes sir, Mr. Phelps, I'm on it. Breathe in underwater and
out above water, right?"

"That doesn't sound right to me," said Audrey.

"It's not, I was just testing my sensei."

"Well, you failed that one," said Trey. "Don't be afraid, I also learned CPR from Darell."

"Then kiss me, you fool!" Richard said a little too loudly as Dr. Cole entered the room.

"Bad timing?" said the doctor.

"Not the best," responded Audrey. "It's okay, I know about them."

"I promise I won't ask or tell," said Dr. Cole.

"Good news?" asked Trey.

"Afraid not," was the serious response. Turning to Trey, "Before I share the details, I want you to know that I haven't lost any confidence in our ability to address the situation, but our work will be much more involved than anticipated and recovery will be weeks, not days.

"We were hoping for a simple laparoscopic extraction, but the blood tests and CT scan were telling us otherwise. An initial scope confirms that she tried to downplay a lot of serious pain, which led to a rupture. When the appendix bursts, there is often a sudden relief from the pain. In the worst-case scenario, a patient will believe all is well and further ignore the precipitating events while digestive juices and bacteria begin to flood the abdomen.

"The inflammatory reaction to that causes peritonitis. The digestive juices begin to perforate the surrounding organs and tissues, which triggers a defensive formation of pus-filled abscesses, confirmed present by a CT scan.

"Her temperature, heart rate, respiratory rate, and white blood cell counts are all elevated, especially the white blood count, and her arterial CO2 level is lowered. That, and our initial look with the scope, indicates widespread bacteria and a septic condition that needs immediate aggressive action. We've already started the associated antibiotics, and we are moving now to an open surgery environment to address the need for a thorough cleansing of the abdominal cavity to remove any lingering infectious materials.

"Trey, I hope I'm not overwhelming you or scaring you, but I want you to know we are dealing with the worst of the worst-case scenario. I still have complete confidence that the path already in progress will arrest and address your wife's current situation and lead to a full recovery."

"Got it," said Trey. "You're my hero."

"Not Michael Strahan?"

"Not funny at all."

"We will be leaving a scar that won't be covered by hair this time, unless Vicki plans to sport a substantial belly toupee."

"Please keep your day job."

"I'll check back in with our progress report in the next hour."

Trey reached for his hand and pulled him in for one of those awkward man hugs. "Thank you, Dr. Cole."

"Anytime, see you all soon."

"Not the best news," said Audrey

"I don't know," said Richard. "I got a little chuckle about the belly toupee thing."

Trey shot him a look. "It's a good thing Darell couldn't make it. One insensitive bastard at a time is about my limit."

"I suppose I should call Darell again and update him," said Audrey.

"I appreciate that. If you two don't mind holding the fort, I'm going to visit the chapel for a bit."

Audrey made the call.

"Darell sends more hugs and prayers. I should probably also check in with Michele and let her know this may be some time."

"Hello."

"Hi Michele, it's Audrey."

"Hi Audrey, any news yet?"

"The doctor says things will turn out okay, but it's more involved than they hoped for. It may be a lot longer than we thought. What time do you need to leave? I can have Richard drop me off."

"I never need to leave as far as I'm concerned. The shop is a little slow right now so Michael's okay as a one-man show."

"Are you sure?"

"Absolutely. Plus, I couldn't have any better company or entertainment than Elizabeth and Lincoln. She is the best baby ever, and the two of them are the cutest pair."

"I'm guessing she hasn't pooped yet," Audrey laughed.

Michele also laughed. "Oh no, she's quite productive, but I'm not a first timer and I still have COVID masks around. I don't guess I'll be having any more kids, but if I did, I'd want one exactly like Elizabeth. Really, we're fine here. Take care of Vicki and Trey. I can stay as long as you need."

"Thanks, Michele, we'll keep you posted."

"See ya."

It was over two hours of waiting when Dr. Cole returned.

"My apologies for leaving you hanging. I got pulled away on another emergency."

"Is Vicki okay?" asked Audrey

"Yes, she'll be fine. Her procedure went according to plan, and she's recovering now. I need to get back to this other patient. Trey, I can get you into the recovery room on the way so you can be there when Vicki wakes up. We should have her in a private room in about another hour, and the rest of you can visit then."

Audrey hugged Trey. "We'll be right here."

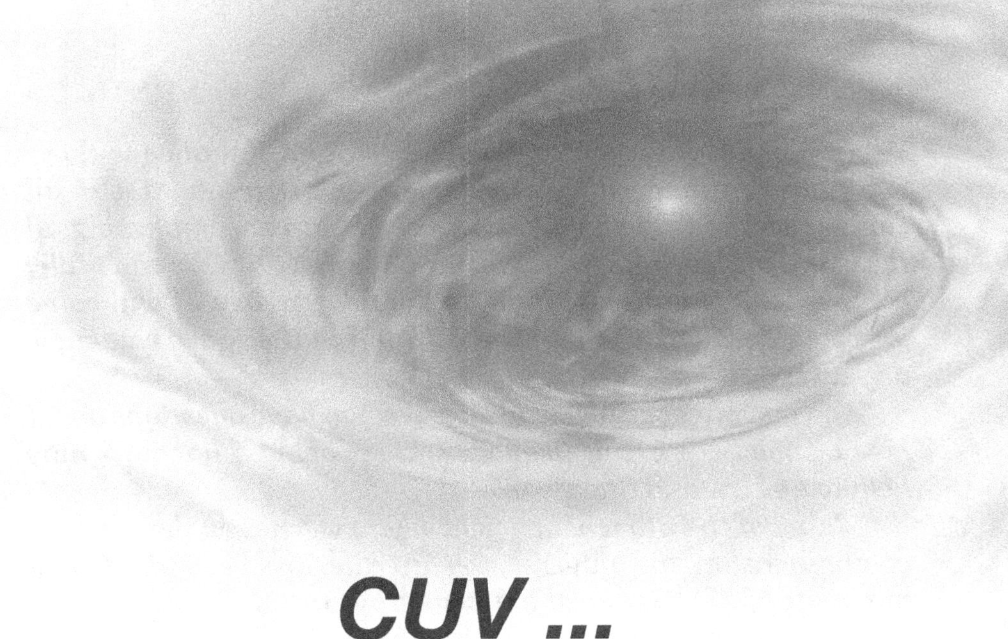

CUV ...

WHAT SHE HAD ONLY KNOWN AS THE NAKED woman from the mist was clear before her, no longer a floating apparition. It wasn't clothed, but it wasn't naked. It was a smooth form like something she had seen in a comic book movie, beautiful in a feminine sense yet also somehow androgynous.

"Isabel?"

"Yes, Vicki."

There was no sound in the Portal, but the shared thought energy was a communication clearer and stronger than anything she'd known in the world.

"I've wanted to be back here."

"I know."

"Am I dead?"

"Just deeper that any natural sleep in the unconscious. You'll go away from here soon, and in time return to physical wellness."

"Did you bring me here?"

Isabel's laugh was like the tinkling bell, an unexpected sensory prompt in the silent realm.

"I wish I had that power."

"Then how am I here?"

"In a small way, you're always here, and I'm always there. We have a primary state of being here or there, but we're all connected like drops in a sort of vast ocean encompassing all the world and the afterworld in one body of water. We can't fully comprehend it until we've made the full journey. It will come for you someday, but that time is far off in the space you know as years.

"You and our special friend Don Weston have questions about how I came to be in this primary state of being. That story may help to understand the ocean.

"Think of the Stonehenge field where we met as the whole of comprehension, the universe, the afterlife, and beyond. My last moments of life happened in the nearby barn. I died from knife wounds that opened me up inside and out until my blood was drained. Other tools dismembered my dead body to small pieces that were burned to ash in an oven.

"Chips of remaining bone were crushed to dust in a press. All of that was mixed with sands of dried clay and scattered across that field. My physical being became tiny specks that now inhabit the ground that represents the whole of comprehension, the universe, the afterlife, and beyond. All our souls, living or dead, always exist like that. In tiny specks ever-present in all conscious and unconscious realms."

"Wow."

"So, you get it?"

"I think so."

"I wish we had met and become friends when I was alive. We connect well."

"I have so many questions. I think I'm clear that the primary home for the living will always be the physical earth. You've helped me understand how I got here, but what makes the difference between being in the Portal or in the full light? I was never able to pass that final barrier."

"There is some choice. Even in my state, I don't fully understand how you're here now, but I knew you'd come back. In your first visit, you were indeed dead to get here, but your friends brought you back before the final passage.

"Many choose the final passage once. Those are the fortunate ones who die at the right time for them. They are at peace that passing is near, and they are at peace with their spiritual state. They are anxious for the beyond and go straight to the light."

"The streaks I've seen that fly past us?"

"Yes!"

"And the rest?"

"The rest are like me. We weren't ready. In death we go through the final passage to the light. It's wonderful and peaceful there, but the Portal remains open to all the dead. The streaks are the blessed ones who can remain content through eternity. The rest of us wander back and forth with lingering troubles in our souls, unfinished business in a sense.

"Some can almost touch the world, maybe even enough to be thought of as a ghost, or even a poltergeist. Some, like the George Bailey story, may even find a way to earn their peace and readiness to join the light forever. Many, like those who die by suicide, may never find true rest."

"Is that the end for Glenn Weaver?"

"Maybe. But because he is here, there is always hope. The truly evil souls never make it to the Portal or the light."

"Where do they go when they die?"

"You'll find when you get here that you don't need or want to know. But we do know what they were, and they aren't with us."

"Thinking back to the George Bailey story, can you help with what you told us about Elizabeth being in danger? Was it because she was outside of the circle at the séance?"

"She has her own protection from that. She can't express it yet in the mortal world, but she was born with the gift. I'm certain Elizabeth is why you've been able to come here again. The two of you are linked forever from your first meeting before her birth. Your growth together in that relationship will be profound as you learn to trust the guidance of a higher power."

"I'll teach her everything I know."

"What you know now is incomplete for that task. You'll learn more, but the lessons will be hard. Sadly, there has already begun *a series of unfortunate events leading to a time where Elizabeth will be taken away by someone."*

"Can we prevent that? Do you know who is going to take her?"

"Yes."

"So, we can stop them and save Elizabeth?"

Vicki was shocked as she suddenly felt a very human need to urinate.

NO!

"WAKEY WAKEY," TREY WAS SAYING PLAY-
fully as he stroked Vicki's hand. "Welcome back."

Vicki could see the shape of a clock on the wall coming into focus. Trey was startled as her eyes opened wide and her face contorted in sheer terror. She rasped, "No, no, I can't be here," barely audible coming from her dry mouth and lips.

"Are you okay? Are you in pain?"

"No, I have to go back," still almost unintelligible as she started to struggle.

"Nurse, please!" yelled Trey. "My wife is in trouble."

Multiple bodies in scrubs appeared quickly. "I need you to step away. We know how to take care of her."

"She's my wife."

"I know, and she'll be fine shortly, this is not uncommon, and we're trained to deal with it. I need you to step into the hall so we can take care of her."

Vicki was moaning and crying aloud, "I have to go back. I need to know what she was going to tell me."

"Please try to relax. You're in the recovery room. You're out of surgery." They had to hold her down now.

"I can't be here. Someone I know is in trouble, and I'm the only one who can help her."

"When you're fully awake you'll be better, and you can help them then."

Tears flowing, "You can't understand." Still muffled, "I can only help if I can go back to sleep. Let me go back."

The attendants continued holding her down and telling her things like "This happens" and "Everything is going to be fine" and "You're all better now." Vicki became fully awake and stopped struggling, resigning to the truth that she wouldn't be going back now.

The nurse brought Trey back to her. "I love you, Vicki. Please don't cry, everything is going to be okay. What can I do to make it better?"

Alert and focused now. "I need to talk to Audrey."

Dr. Cole heard the last of this as he had joined Trey at the bedside. He had been alerted by the recovery nurse.

"Vicki," he said, concerned. "How are you doing?"

"Oh, thank God you're here." She was excited and anxious. "I have to go back."

"Back where?"

"Back to sleep. I have to go back now."

"Vicki, you're going to be all well now, your surgery was a complete success, and your recovery is already underway. What you are experiencing now is not uncommon. You're having an episode of what we call emergence delirium. It will pass soon, and you'll not even remember it occurred."

"I must remember! Elizabeth is in danger."

Dr. Cole looked to Trey. "Elizabeth is Audrey's baby?"

"Yes."

"Nurse, 2 mg lorazepam please. Vicki, I'm going to give you something that will help reduce your anxiety."

"Will it put me back to sleep? Please, I have to go back for Elizabeth."

"I know you want to talk to Audrey. I think that might be helpful. If you take this now, it will calm you so we can move to a room where Audrey can visit."

"Please, it's important that I go back now."

"We can't go back now. It's too soon. But we can discuss it further when you're feeling better." He'd tell her anything now that might help her relax.

Vicki took the pill.

"Close your eyes and think about visiting with Audrey. We'll have you together soon. I'll let Audrey know you're looking forward to seeing her. Trey will stay with you until we can move you to your room."

Trey was stroking her hand again and talking softly as Dr. Cole left to go to the waiting area. Darell had joined Richard and Audrey there.

Darell was laughing as he greeted Dr. Cole with a handshake and "I just got here so no one can blame me for any broken ribs this time."

The doctor didn't return the laugh.

"Oh no," said Audrey. "Is something wrong?"

"Vicki is having some anxiety reaction in coming out of the anesthesia. It's not uncommon and wouldn't be a concern but for the fact that she didn't have such a reaction previously. We've already given her something that will calm her quickly, and it will pass. She should be settled in her room in about half an hour."

"Can we see her then?" asked Richard.

"Yes, but I think you should greet her alone first," he said to Audrey. "She's been having some delusions about your daughter and asked for you specifically. I think it would be a good thing if you were there for her. It's entirely possible that she won't have any memory of her episode by then, but if she does, you can help her work it out."

Audrey agreed. She knew there was more to Vicki's state of mind that the doctor couldn't possibly understand.

TELL ME

AUDREY WAS ALREADY IN THE ROOM WHEN Vicki was wheeled in by the attendant. The door closed and they were alone.

"I saw her," said Vicki. "I saw Isabel. It was her that we talked to. She died at the barn, and I know every detail. She was carved up and burned and crushed into dust. Her remains are scattered in the Stonehenge field."

"I believe you."

"She had news about Elizabeth. She said she was in danger, not from the séance but something else."

"Tell me," said Audrey, holding Vicki's hand.

"I have to go back, there's more to know," she said with tears in her eyes. "I was so selfish in wanting to learn more about the Portal. I wasted time talking about ghosts and angels and even Glenn Weaver. I woke up too soon. I never heard the last answer that might save Elizabeth. I promised, and I let you down. I must go back."

"You could never let me down, Vicki. What do you know? What do we need to save Elizabeth from?"

"She's going to be kidnapped."

"Kidnapped! By whom?"

"I don't know. That's why I need to go back right away. Isabel knows. I have to find out what she was about to tell me when I woke up."

There was a knock at the door, and Dr. Cole stuck his head in the room. "How are you doing, Vicki?"

"Sad."

"You had a bit of a troubling reaction coming out of the anesthesia. We also used a fairly new approach to pain management with something called an ESP block. That shouldn't have been a complicating factor, but I do want to keep it in mind as we work through this. How is your pain level from the surgery?"

"The pain is okay, but I wasn't ready to come back. I wasn't finished."

"Can we talk about it?"

"Do you believe in miracles?"

"Vicki, I see them every day. Yes, I believe."

"Do you believe there's a place we go when we die?"

"I do."

"I've been to that place. Twice now. Can you put me back there?"

"I'm not sure I understand." Dr. Cole looked at Audrey. She seemed to understand.

"A doctor friend of mine, not an MD but an academic doctor, told me she read an article about people having out-of-body experiences from ketamine. Did you use ketamine to put me to sleep?"

"No, we use propofol, but there are many journal articles on such experiences from both drugs and other anesthetics. Is that the experience that troubles you?"

"It doesn't trouble me. It enlightens me. When I go to that place, I meet others who have passed, and I know things that are going to happen."

"How so?"

"I don't really know, but the messages are clear to me."

"My medical opinion tells me that our subconscious tries to sort out dreams of things we don't understand."

"These aren't dreams," in a raised voice. "This is real."

"It's okay, Vicki," said the doctor softly. "My non-medical opinion tells me there are things we'll never understand in our time here. I know enough about you that I believe your experience could be genuine."

"Then you'll help me to go back?"

"What exactly are you hoping I can do?"

"I need you to give me the drugs that can take me back to the Portal. I have to find out what someone there was trying to tell me."

"Vicki, I can't do that even if I wanted to, and I wouldn't want to. I'm sure your police friend Darell could give you some history on how these drugs are entering the recreational world and the black market along with other fatality-inducing bad ideas like fentanyl. What you're asking me to do is quite serious, even with strict medical observation in a controlled environment."

"But it would be okay if you supervised it."

"No, it wouldn't be okay to administer powerful anesthetics without a medical purpose."

"Do you think I'm crazy?"

"I don't think you have the capacity to be crazy. I think you are mere hours post-op from a life-threatening surgery and you're suffering some lingering anxiety from the trauma. I don't believe you're crazy, and I do believe what you've experienced is very real to you. I don't want you to think I'm ignoring that or writing it off, but you need to get some rest, and we can talk again tomorrow. Can we do that?"

Vicki was tired.

"I think Dr. Cole is right, Vicki, and we should listen to him," said Audrey.

"I'm going to keep you on the lorazepam through the night. Your pain block will wear off by morning. Don't hesitate to ask for additional relief if you become uncomfortable. Sleep is your friend right now, and we'll reconvene to look for solutions to your other lingering concerns in the morning."

"You'll help me go back?"

"We'll look for solutions. For now, my prescription is a quick visit from Trey and your friends followed by a night of rest. Do you understand?"

Audrey repeated herself, "I think Dr. Cole is right. Let's get you some rest."

"I am tired," said Vicki. "Okay."

As Dr. Cole left to send in the visitors, he turned at the door and mouthed *"thank you"* to Audrey.

EVERYBODY NEEDS A GOOD NIGHT'S SLEEP

TREY, RICHARD, DARELL, AND AUDREY obeyed the guidance for a quick visit and then followed each other back to the Craft house. No food plans tonight, everyone was beat.

Audrey made a call on the way, and Michele greeted the group as they arrived. "You all look tired. You didn't have to come back on my account. I'm ready to move in and keep Elizabeth and Lincoln forever."

"Thanks, Michele," said Richard. "We're glad you could do it."

"I can do it anytime. It really is a treat for me. I felt like a real mother to the best kids in the world."

"We're trying to decide if we're having beer or wine for dinner tonight," said Trey. "Will you join us?"

"Not tonight. I'm going to grab some carryout for Michael on my way back to the shop so I can pick him up and head home. We'll see you there in the morning."

Michele headed out, and the group conscience voted on wine for dinner. Darell and Trey gave Lincoln some frisbee time before he settled in against Elizabeth on their floor mattress in the great room. It was a weary group as everyone else collapsed on the comfy furniture there and Richard started a fire in the fireplace.

"She went back to the Portal," said Audrey. "Isabel told her Elizabeth is going to be kidnapped. She woke up before she found out who will do it."

Everyone remained silent. Richard broke that with, "Do we believe that?"

"I do," from Audrey.

Trey now, "I think I do too. She was really stressed when she woke up. She kept saying she had to go back."

"When she and I were with Dr. Cole in her room, she kept saying the same thing and pleading with him to give her the drugs to do it. She's serious. He finally convinced her to get some rest and said they'd talk more tomorrow."

Darell asked, "Do you think he's considering it?"

"Definitely not, and he made that clear. I think he's hoping she'll get over her reaction to the surgery and forget all about it in the morning ... I don't think she will."

"She won't," said Trey. "I know she won't."

"What do we do now?" asked Richard of the group.

"Nothing," said Darell. "We wait and see how things develop. If Isabel is real and has answers, as I know some of us believe, we'd like to have those answers, but not at any risk to Vicki."

"She's desperate and serious about taking any risk. She feels like she let us down," Audrey said.

"I don't want to lose her again," said Trey. "I can't let her go back when she might never return. I can't do this."

"You're right," said Darell. "None of us can do this. Vicki has a strong will, and we have to all be on board to protect her from that."

Looking at Elizabeth, Richard said, "We all need some rest. Let's see if Dr. Cole can make another miracle tomorrow."

TOMORROW, TOMORROW

DARELL WAS AT THE HOSPITAL EARLY THE next day, stopping in on the way to his shift. He brought a life-sized stuffed sheltie with him. He'd ordered it from Amazon for Elizabeth but thought it might be more appropriate for Vicki first. She was awake but still a little sleepy when he entered the room.

"All better?" he said cheerily.

"You know it. Who's your friend?"

"A gift from Lincoln since he's not allowed to visit. He said you should hold it tight when you cough or laugh. I'm here to make you laugh."

"Then do it already, I could use a laugh."

"Did you hear about the new study that recently found that humans eat more bananas than monkeys?"

"I can't say that I have."

"It's true. I can't remember the last time I ate a monkey."

"Mmmm, good try but not exactly a thigh slapper or a stuffed dog hugger."

"Maybe I'm not at my funniest today. I had a minor car accident on the way here."

"Really? Are you okay?"

"I'm fine but it was my fault. I was checking a text and rear-ended a guy at a light. Not a big hit, but he got out of the car to check. It turns out he was a 'person of short stature,' a dwarf. He told me he wasn't happy."

"I guess not."

"I responded, 'Well which one are you then?'"

After a second, Vicki reached for the dog and giggled, "You got me on that one."

"Better now?"

"A little bit, see what I did there?" Another giggle and another squeeze of the dog. "Wow, it does hurt to laugh. I need a serious moment. Can you call Don Weston for me?"

"Certainly, he should be sitting on his porch with a cigar and coffee about now. I let him know about your condition last night," he said. He made the call and handed her the phone. "I'm sure he'd appreciate hearing your voice with a positive update."

"What's up, you rat bastard?" answered Don.

"I love you too," said Vicki.

"Vicki, sorry I thought …"

"I know," she interrupted. "He's right here, and he is a rat bastard."

"You sound much better than the report I got yesterday."

"Darell can be such a drama queen. I'm doing fine."

"Good to know, I was just thinking about making a field trip to check on you."

"I'd love to see you, but I have news that may give you plenty of field work right where you are."

"Oh, what's that?"

"I saw Isabel again. During my surgery, she had answers for you."

"About?"

"Her death. She was murdered at the barn and never left there."

"Did she say how?"

"She said she was bled to death, dismembered, and cremated. Her bones were crushed, and everything was mixed in some sort of clay sand and scattered on the Stonehenge field."

Long silence.

"What are you thinking?" Vicki asked.

"A thousand things at once. That would explain why we never found a conventional trace of her. It may also give us directions to look for more. I'm glad it's still an open crime scene for a missing person case. I'd never be able to get a fresh warrant by explaining how I got this new information."

"Then you do believe me, that I saw Isabel?"

"I'm not sure what to believe anymore, but I don't doubt your senses, and it's easy enough to check for new evidence. I'll start today and keep you informed. I'll also let Abbey know what's going on down there. You take care of yourself. Give everyone a hug for me, and we'll talk soon." He signed off.

"That sounded positive," said Darell, taking the phone. "So, how was your night? I'm guessing there's some pain on the menu."

"Manageable. They gave me some pills and a morphine drip. I get to trigger it, but it has a limit. Maybe we can figure out how to override it. It's good enough for the pain but not enough to get me where I need to be."

"I knew where you wanted to get to even before the call with Don. Audrey told us about your visit with Isabel."

"I knew she would. There's more to know if I can just talk to Isabel again. It's the drugs that get me there, but I don't think Dr. Cole is going to give them to me."

"As he shouldn't."

"He said you would probably know about the black market for them."

"More than I wish I did. We have an evidence room full of that stuff, but I'm pretty sure he wasn't suggesting that I should get them there for you."

"No, but why not? We know that propofol works, and ketamine also might do it. It sounds like people take those for fun all the time without problems."

"You think so? You've already had a problem with the one that killed Michael Jackson and now you think you'd like to try the one that killed Matthew Perry? And they were both supposed to be under medical supervision. What makes you'd think you'd be safe without that?"

"I wouldn't be taking them for fun. I'd be taking them for Elizabeth. There's no other way to get the answers."

"Vicki. I love you. I believe in you. I even believe you've met Isabel. But I'm not going to help you get propofol or ketamine or try to break your morphine drip to see if that will send you back to the land of the dead. We have to find another way, or we just have to deal with circumstances if and when they occur."

"Part of me knows you're right, but the rest of me can't give up trying."

"I know. I need to get to work now, but I can't leave until you promise me you'll be okay."

"Faux Lincoln is here to protect me. I'm okay."

Darell went to the parking lot where he got into Trey's truck parked next to his cruiser. "It's worse than Audrey told us. She wanted me to get her propofol or ketamine to send her back to the Portal."

Trey didn't say anything.

"She seriously thought I might do it."

"You wouldn't, would you?"

"Hell no."

"I'm afraid of losing her. She won't give up on this."

"Maybe she'll come back to her senses in a few days."

"These are her senses. As long as I've known her, she's had a call to this paranormal search. She's found a way to get there and a reason she must go back. She won't give up."

"The one saving grace is that there is no way she can get these drugs on her own, and there's no one we know that will get them for her ... I need to check in at work, and you need to go love your wife."

"I won't tell her we talked."

"Agreed. Good luck."

Trey found Vicki sleeping peacefully when he entered the room. He stretched out the recliner by the bed and closed his eyes, not sleeping but trying to calm his mind. They both opened their eyes when Dr. Cole showed up.

"It looks like everyone is still alive in here. That's a good sign. On the one to ten scale, how is your pain level?"

"If I say one can I go home?"

"Afraid not. We think we got ahead of your infection, but it will be a few days before we can confirm that in your white blood cell count. Did you sleep okay?"

"I rested between pills and tests."

"Rest is your best friend right now. Who's that new friend you're hugging?"

Vicki gave the dog a squeeze. "This is from Darell and Lincoln. Can I keep him, Daddy, if I promise to walk him every day and pick up his poops?"

"You're remarkably precocious for someone that went through what you did yesterday. That's good."

"You said we'd look at solutions to help me get back to the Portal. That's good too, so I'm optimistic. What have you come up with? I'm ready to go."

"Whoa, Secretariat, I said we'd look for solutions to your concerns. That's a little different."

"I only have one concern, and that's it."

"Let's start with telling me about this Portal, how you got there, what it is, and why you feel you must go back."

"It's that place between life and the light of death, and I got there when I died. I couldn't go all the way into the light because I didn't stay dead, but I was still in the Portal where all souls pass moving between here and there."

"Between life and death?"

"Yes."

"There are gaps between medical science and spirituality that can't be explained, although a lot of credible research has tried to. I deal with death and near-death patients all the time, and their stories have always fascinated me. They bring an almost universal message of out-of-body experience, the light, and the tunnel. A few have feared what happened to them, but the vast majority, like you, have found the experience to be peaceful and pleasant and expressed a desire to return someday. Tell me why it seems so important to you to return now."

"Audrey's daughter Elizabeth is in danger. She is going to be kidnapped. There is a woman in the Portal who told me this. I woke up as she was about to tell me who was going to take Elizabeth."

Dr. Cole looked at Trey for any sign of disbelief. There was none. The doctor pondered what he just heard and was conflicted in his thoughts. He believed her too.

"I understand your urgency then. I am interested in learning more about your Portal encounters, but you need to recover from your surgery first. You're going to be here for a few days at least, and we'll visit every morning. I'll bring my scientific brain to monitor your physical process. I'll bring the rest of me to continue our current conversation, if that's okay with you."

"I'd like that."

"Trey, is it okay with you if I reserve the 8:00–10:00 a.m. visiting slot for the next few days?"

"Sure, I'll alert the troops to sleep in."

"I have more rounds to make. She's all yours."

"Thanks, I think."

DR. PHIL

VICKI WOULD SPEND FIVE DAYS IN THE HOS-pital. Her pain levels and surgical healing went well, and she was due to be released as the blood tests confirmed that infection was arrested. As promised, Dr. Cole visited every morning. Like Vicki's friend Abbey, he was a trained scientist but had seen too much that science couldn't explain in his medical practice. The actual wound healing process was always magical to him, and his ICU experience with so many near-death patients had made him a secret believer in the paranormal/spiritual realm that Vicki had steeped in most of her life.

Day Two post op: "Good morning, any unexpected pain or discomfort we need to take a look at?"

"No, and I slept well too."

"Good, that concludes our medical session. I'm ready to suspend all scientific skepticism and delve into the mystic with you. Tell me all about the Portal."

Vicki talked for the next hour, only interrupted by the occasional "Hmmm" or brief clarifying questions. She told him the whole story about the first visit, transporting quickly to the light but not being able to cross over. He found absolute lucidity as she listed everyone she encountered there and what transpired. The description of the Stonehenge séance and reuniting with the mysterious form that turned out to be Isabel's initial warning was the biggest "Hmmm."

"Isabel told you then she'd see you soon?"

"And she did, just two days ago, in the Portal. I've tried in my sleep to get back there, but I can only make it to the foggy edge where I see shapes but can't communicate. It's the really deep sleep of the surgery that got me back."

"Tell me about that most recent journey."

She did, again with completely believable precision and certainty. The details of Isabel's death, the talk of suicides and tortured souls wandering from the light to the mist of the Portal, and finally the compelling warning of a pending kidnapping and the return to consciousness before getting the next answer that could help.

"I see why you want to go back."

"Even if I didn't want to, I have to. Can you get me what I need to go back?"

"I admire your tenacity, but we already covered that ground. Can we shift gears just a bit? I shared your story with a colleague of mine who has the same interest in where patients go in near-death or return-from-death encounters. His specialty is psychiatry. Would it be okay if I bring him by tomorrow to continue our exploration?"

"You do think I'm crazy."

"Not at all. Nor does he. In fact, he's familiar with your personal background and would love to meet you and learn more. He's authored a number of journal papers on patients' afterlife experiences, and he finds you to be an extraordinarily and uniquely gifted subject to inform and expand that topic."

"Which makes me some kind of guinea pig experiment to him?"

"I think if you agree to meet him, you'll find otherwise. He considers you to be a subject matter expert in a poorly documented realm that he thinks has great importance, and I agree with him. He wants to meet you not for study but for collaboration in studies. If it's okay with you, I'd like to fill him in on our conversation today and bring him around to continue it with us tomorrow."

Vicki weighed options. It could be interesting, and it's not like she had anything better to do with the time. "Sure, why not."

"We'll see you in the morning. You'll like him."

The rest of Vicki's day was split between visitors and naps. Trey had let the group know about the 8:00–10:00 Cole reservation, and Audrey volunteered to coordinate times for the rest of them.

Day Three post-op: "Good morning, Vicki, any medical concerns?"

"Fit as a fiddle, but my belly itches."

"That's a good sign on the sutures healing. We'll get you some relief for that. I've got Dr. Thomas Justice waiting outside if you're ready to meet him."

"Doctor? the name sounds like he should have been a lawyer."

"He's far too human for that."

"I guess I'm ready. Does this gown make me look fat?"

"It's quite fetching as a complement to the no makeup and no hairbrush look. He's seen worse."

Vicki's first impression was that Dr. Justice looked a lot like Dr. Phil. She hoped he'd be more like Dr. Phil from the Oprah days rather than whatever the current version was.

"I hear you're human," opened Vicki.

"Last I checked. I've been looking forward to meeting the legendary Mrs. Roadcap."

"Vicki."

"Call me Tom."

"I didn't know I was legendary."

"You are to me. I've been to the Peacock Plume several times but always missed you."

"I didn't know I had a stalker, seems like I should have sensed that," she said with a giggle.

"My research interest in the spiritual and paranormal lends itself to stalking. I was aware of your abilities as I followed the local news on your exploits at the Civil War Hospital last year. Dr. Cole has told me about your death and recovery, your description of the Portal, and the more recent séance story. If anyone can help fill the holes in my research, it would be you. I'm happy to finally meet you in person."

"Likewise, I'm sure."

"I'm very impressed with the collection in your store, especially the extensive library. It's easy to find the spooky stuff, but you've also gathered a nice selection of the skeptical and scientific. I've bought several volumes from you that have helped broaden my research."

"Then I can assume you were one of the buyers of Bennett's *Parapsychology: Science of the Paranormal?*"

"You may assume correctly. It's one of the better examples of how to have an open-minded look at bridging the explainable and unexplainable without crapping on either view."

"I do like him," said Vicki to Dr. Cole.

"Good. Then I'll leave the two of you to explore your common interests and let Tom be your wake-up call tomorrow as well. I'm going to take a well-deserved day of R&R. When I return all refreshed, we may be able to get you out of here."

VICKI AND TOM

TOM CONTINUED THE CONVERSATION AFTER Dr. Cole left. "Bennett's look at near-death experiences and altered consciousness is especially of interest to me. The death experience is novel for every one of us. Expectations of the end of life may vary for the geriatric, the hospice bound, and the trauma of the ICU, but I've been exposed to too many similarities of patient-reported experiences across the spectrum to not believe there is something there beyond scientific explanation. I'm especially interested in what I hear you've seen."

"Am I breaking the mold?"

"Initially, no, but you go far beyond it. And you're a credible witness to me. You're well versed in the study of the paranormal, and you have a proven track record of surfacing information not otherwise available through conventional channels. How do you make sense of the gifts you seem to have?"

"It's always made sense to me because I didn't know anything else growing up. As early as I can remember, I've had hints or intuitive nudges of things that might happen before they occurred. And then they did occur. I didn't realize that was not normal until I was in junior high school. A boy was missing from classes for several days, and the parents and police came to the school. I knew he had just run away from home and was hiding in the woods. I don't know how I knew that, but I was able to take them to him. I was surprised because I thought everyone knew what I knew."

"It's odd that your family hadn't noticed before that."

"I didn't really have a family. I never knew a father, and my first memories were moving from shelter to shelter with my mother. She died when I was eight, and I went from foster care to foster care after that. I also thought all of that was normal until other kids began to tease me about it. I kept to myself after that, until the thing with the missing boy."

"What changed after that?"

"The school librarian, Mrs. Monahan, adopted me, not literally, but she took me under her wing. She asked me if I knew the boy and how I knew where he was. I told her the truth that I didn't really know him, but he was one of the few students who was nice to me. We'd never really talked, but he'd wave and say hi if he saw me. She thought maybe I had a relationship with him and maybe even helped him run away and find a hiding place. She was checking me out to see if I really had ESP. She believed in such things."

"Interesting."

"She gave me the book *Edgar Casey on ESP*, which is when I first discovered that my normal wasn't so normal after all. It scared me at first, but Mrs. Monahan told me I had a gift, a gift she wished she had. One that we should keep to ourselves until we fully understand the power of it. She said I shouldn't fear it, but I should be cautious about how I use it and test it carefully."

"Did she help you test it?"

"She had a deck of the Zener cards. It was a bunch of repeated symbols. You shuffled the deck and made a guess at the next card."

"I'm familiar with them. How did you do?"

"From the start I rarely missed a guess. She also tried just picking one out and thinking about it to see if I could name it. I always got those ones."

"I doubt I'd get a single one," said Tom laughing.

"Do you keep in touch with Mrs. Monahan?"

"We only had one year together. We read a lot more on ESP, telepathy, spirits, séances, clairvoyance, precognition, and the tools and protection awareness of the tarot, Ouija, and séances. She also introduced me to oils and crystals."

"Why only one year?"

"Cancer, she had less than two months from diagnosis to death."

"Did you sense that was coming?"

"I knew."

"But you didn't tell her?"

"It wouldn't change anything."

"Do you feel like there was unfinished business in that relationship?"

"I'll always miss her but, looking back, no. In my time with her she gave me everything I needed to understand and research my differences and responsibly accept them. Her job was done, and mine was just starting."

It was 10:00 and Trey popped in.

"Trey, meet Dr. Tom Justice, he's my new shrink," Vicki said as Trey gave her a kiss on the forehead. "Tom, this is my husband, Trey."

Shaking hands with the doctor, Trey said, "I knew you guys would figure out the real problem eventually. You can be honest with me. Looney tunes, right?"

"Worst case I've seen," the doctor laughed. "Just kidding, your wife is a unique resource for my research agenda on near-death experience."

"I'm trying to break her of her own research there. Are you sure a prescription for a straitjacket wouldn't be a good call? She's quite a handful for me unrestrained."

"I thought we weren't going to tell anyone about the whips and handcuffs," said Vicki with a straight face.

"See what I mean?"

"Nice to meet you, Trey, but I think this is where I bow out of the conversation. Vicki, we're at a good stopping point?"

"I think so."

"Great, then let's call it a day so you can have your visitors and continue your physical recovery. Tomorrow I'd like to come back to learn more about the afterlife experience."

"I'll be ready."

DAY FOUR
POST-OP

A LIGHT RAP ON THE DOOR, AND TOM entered asking the physician question, "Any medical concerns this morning?"

"Healthy as a horse."

"I'll see if I can get an alfalfa treat added to lunch today."

Checking over his notes, he started with, "Dr. Cole has filled me in on his version of your story from the time he first saw you through your rough awakening after your most recent surgery. I'd like to hear all of that from you."

"Then you know Dr. Cole believes I was clinically dead as a result of a water-skiing accident before he saw me."

"Yes."

"That was when I went to the Portal."

"You saw the light."

"Yes. I was scared at first because I didn't think I was ready to die, but when I began to pass through the light, all was peaceful and good. I was just about to take the last step when something pulled me back to the Portal."

"Help me understand the place you call the Portal."

"It's like a tunnel of soft luminous fog. It's the channel that all souls pass through coming or going. When I'm there, I can drift through it and explore. I can visit with people I have known or known of. You don't have actual conversations, but you do share thoughts that are just as clear."

"Do you think this what a Catholic might call limbo?"

"No, because I learned from Isabel that a soul can come back from beyond the light to visit the Portal. The soul of the dead can stay in the light or wander in the Portal all the way to the edge of the living and sometimes reach beyond, but the Portal space is not a confinement, it's a choice."

"I believe from my notes that you first met Isabel as a result of a séance."

"Yes and no. On my first visit to the Portal, there was a shadowy figure of a woman who followed near me. I learned in the séance that it was Isabel. She said we would meet again. The second meeting was my next visit to the Portal when she let me know Audrey's daughter Elizabeth was in danger."

"That would be the kidnapping warning."

"Yes. Isabel knows who the kidnapper is, but I came back too soon to learn the name. That's why I must go back. Do you believe me?"

"Vicki, I think I do."

"Then can you arrange to send me back?"

"I think you know the answer to that. There is no medically ethical path to do that."

"Can't you say I'm crazy and need to be sedated?"

"No," he responded firmly, then softening. "But even if I did, psychiatric sedation wouldn't introduce the anesthetic medications that brought you there in the past."

"Poop," Vicki pouted. The room was quiet.

Tom spoke first, "Vicki, why do you think Isabel was following you on your first visit?"

"I don't know. We do have a mutual friend, Don Weston."

"I remember that name from last year's news. I believe he was a Civil War historian. Is that right?"

"One of many. Don arranged for a research team from the University of Pennsylvania to come in for an archeological dig. The lead for that was Abbey Foster. She's an academic scientist but she's also a true believer in paranormal, and she has the gift for it. We found an instant connection."

"How might that relate to meeting Isabel?"

"Abbey joined Audrey and me for a Ouija séance. It made for a strong team and an unusually productive encounter, even including a sign from a poltergeist."

"Does Audrey also have the gift?"

"She does. She denies it, but it shows up in her artwork. Still, her skepticism adds to the strength of the group."

"How so?"

"That goes back to Mrs. Monahan's advice that I shouldn't fear the gift, but I should test it carefully. A Ouija séance can surface truths, but it can also surface unconscious influence on truths through the mechanics of the plectrum. Audrey's default to a devil's advocacy is important to maintaining a grounded interpretation. Any skeptic can provide that role, but a gifted one is especially valuable. How this all leads back to Isabel is that Audrey, Abbey, and I were the same team at the Stonehenge séance where Isabel introduced herself."

"This is why your personal story is so important in expanding my research on patient reports of afterlife encounters. You have a life of experience that is not known as normal in our world, and you accept that it should be tempered with skepticism."

"Of course it should be doubted. None of what I'm telling you can be proven."

"Dr. Jeffrey Long would disagree with that."

"Who is he?"

"An oncologist who has studied over 5,000 cases of near-death experience. He believes his research validates life after death. I do too. He established the Near-Death Experience Research Foundation to further that study. I've personally contributed 37 patient interviews to that ongoing investigation. Yours is the most compelling yet. You've died and returned.

You've seen the same light and fog described by so many, and you've felt the peace they speak of. Most accounts end there. You transcend that with descriptions of ongoing exchanges of thought with other spirits through methods both here and beyond. Your background in paranormal studies gives you a unique sense to process the near-death phenomena unlike any other accounts to date. There is whole new volume of knowledge and perspective here that would add much to the field of near-death studies for patients and medical professionals. I think the two of us could write and publish a work on this that would be welcomed and accepted by both peer-reviewed and public sources."

Pause. "You want to write a book with me."

"Yes."

"Wouldn't it be an even better story if you sent me back to the Portal to finish the current chapter?"

Before Tom could respond, Trey and Audrey showed up for the 10:00 a.m. visitor slot.

"Let's both sleep on it," Tom said.

DAY FIVE POST-OP

DRS. COLE AND JUSTICE TAPPED ON VICKI'S door at 7:00 a.m.

"It's about time room service got here with my beignets and coffee."

They entered.

"Apparently no medical concerns this morning," said a smiling Dr. Cole. "I know we don't have beignets, but with a phone call I can get one of my staff to raid the cafeteria for coffee and a big cinnamon bun."

"I guess that will have to do."

He made the call. "You deserve a treat for the excellent blood cell counts you turned in overnight. You've passed your tests with flying colors, and we'll be kicking you back on the street by noon."

"Have you thought about yesterday's conversation?" asked Tom.

"Tom wants us to write a book together," Vicki said to Dr. Cole.

"I heard. I think it would be excellent therapy."

"Possibly," said Vicki, with a little laugh. "Tom needs therapy after spending the past couple of days with me."

"So, you have thought about it. Does that mean you'll do it?" asked Dr. Justice.

"I don't know. Have you thought about my suggestion for ending the current chapter? I'd be willing to grace you with my company for another day or two."

Dr. Cole looked at Dr. Justice quizzically.

"This is my last call," thought Vicki.

Tom said, "Vicki is still trying to convince us to arrange an anesthetic intervention."

The cinnamon bun and coffee arrived. Dr. Cole took the tray to Vicki, saying, "Sorry, Mrs. Roadcap, this wonderful cinnamon bun is as close as you're going to get to heaven today."

"Nothing ventured, nothing gained. I won't ask again," she said, thinking, *"But I'll find a way to do it without you."*

"Thanks," said Tom. "Are you ready to get started on our writing journey?"

"As ready as I know how."

"Good to hear but unfortunately, I'm not ready yet. I'm off to a couple of international conferences over the next month. It will be a good opportunity to hit up colleagues for opinions on our pending publication, but you and I won't be able to reconvene until after that."

"No worries. I honestly am looking forward to the project, but I won't mind getting back to the normal shop routine and studying up on your Dr. Long while you're off to your boondoggles."

"Sounds like Vicki is very familiar with international medical conferences," said Dr. Cole, laughing.

Dr. Justice also had to laugh at that observation. "I'll come by the Peacock Plume on my return, and we can get started."

"Enjoy breakfast," said Dr. Cole. "We're heading out. When today's visitors arrive, they'll be advised that you are fully released medically."

Vicki had some cinnamon bun and a sip of lukewarm coffee. *"Not exactly close to heaven or anywhere else I hoped to be."*

She found her cell phone and called Abbey Foster.

"Vicki! Don told me you were in the hospital. Are you okay?"

"I'd better be because they're kicking me out of here today."

"I hear that Isabel followed up on her promise to see you soon. Don is going to bring in a state evidence tech to revisit the Stonehenge field. I'll be joining that trip. He asked for my input from an archaeological perspective."

"There's more to the Isabel message. Elizabeth is in danger."

"Don didn't tell me that part."

"He didn't know. I only told Audrey at first, but the guys also know now. I guess Darell hasn't told Don either."

"I'm still crushed that I made the mistake of not protecting Elizabeth in the salt circle. I've left Audrey messages by phone and text, but she won't get back to me. I wonder if she'll ever forgive me and talk to me again."

"She will. I've never known her to cut people out of her life or bear a grudge for very long. But I've also never known what the love of a mother for her child feels like. The danger to Elizabeth has nothing to do with the salt circle or spirits from the séance. She is going to be kidnapped."

"No."

"Yes, and I lost the Portal connection before I could find out who or when or anything could help us prevent it. I've begged the doctors to send me back. I know they are believers that there is something there, but without some medical reason for anesthesia, they won't do it."

"What do you think we can do?"

"I don't know yet. I guess for now you can help Don look for the traces of Isabel's body. I'm not giving up on finding another way to get to Isabel's spirit, even if it means fabricating a new medical reason."

Abbey paused. "Vicki, that's not a good thought."

"I know, but it's all I've got right now."

"Promise me you'll not rush into anything that could put you in danger. And stay close to Audrey. She's your kindred spirit and best friend. She can help you have better thoughts."

"You're right. She's my next phone call. I love you and we'll talk again soon. Thanks."

Audrey answered on the first ring. "Everything okay?"

"Good morning to you too."

Audrey laughed, "Sorry, I just knew you were about to call."

"No surprise, after all, you are my kindred spirit, according to Abbey. She says I should stay close to you so I can think better thoughts. I called to let you know Dr. Cole says I can go home today."

"That's certainly a good thought."

"Not really. It means my mission to get him or the shrink to send me back to the Portal is over unless I can come up with a new medical emergency."

"Abbey is right. That's a bad thought."

"You really should call her."

"I've been thinking about that since you told me Isabel said there was no harm to Elizabeth from the séance. I guess I owe her an apology."

"Not for being concerned about your daughter. None of us knew at the time that Elizabeth was truly safe. But maybe for shutting her out and not talking about it. She's been a good friend, and she loves Elizabeth as much as anyone."

"You're thinking better thoughts already," said Audrey. "And I will too. I'll call her soon to patch things up. For now, though, what time should we be bailing you out of your incarceration?"

"The good doctor says noonish."

"Then we'll see you soon. Any cravings for lunch?"

"Chinese please."

Vicki spent the next two hours alone assessing her next steps. *"This won't be over until I am back with Isabel again and get the rest of the information,"* she thought. *"I'll find a way, but I need to be patient and silent. I can't tell anyone about my plans, not the doctors, not Audrey, not even Trey."*

BACK IN PENNSYLVANIA, THE HUNT FOR ISABEL

DON MADE A FIELD TRIP TO GLENN WEAVER'S property and followed up with a call to an old friend, Lieutenant Colonel Lester Timmons, director of the Pennsylvania State Police Bureau of Criminal Investigation based in Harrisburg.

"Lester, I'd like to borrow one of your evidence techs to take another look at our missing person case from Churchville University."

"Really? That must be over a year old. We didn't close that case?"

"Two years and, no, the person is still missing."

"Interesting. What's up?"

"I got some new information on the nature of the death and disposal of the body. There may be a chance to recover some DNA after all."

"How did you come up with that?"

"Not sure you want to know."

"That's cryptic."

"Okay, full disclosure. A psychic source. Would you still be able to help with a resource?"

"It wouldn't be the first time we considered questionable input as an excuse to reexamine an open cold case. Do you know specifically what you're after? It would help to determine who I might send and what tools to have on hand."

"The word on the street is that our victim was dismembered and cremated at the Weaver barn scene. The bones were crushed, and all the remains were mixed with some sort of dry clay and scattered in a field. I was up there this morning. With a little raking I was able to turn up some granules of what looks like kitty litter or oil-dry absorbent."

"How big is the search area?"

"Probably less than an acre."

"Do you have access to 110- or 220-volt power at the scene?"

"Negative."

"No problem, I'll send a generator with the tech and the vacuum."

"Vacuum?"

"Vacuum. It's specially designed for sweeping small particulates in an open field environment."

"No shit. Who would have thought that up."

"Likely the first forensic examiner faced with a similar search need. It's also quite good for interior use on capturing trace evidence. I don't know how effective we'll be working in a two-year-old open environment, but it's worth a try. If the grains you're seeing actually are some form of clay absorbent, the odds are not bad that we may be able to extract something of value, especially if we can gather a decent sample of them. When do you want to start?"

"What's your guy doing tomorrow? I'm up early."

"Can he meet you at your campus office at 7:00 a.m. tomorrow? As I recall, we'll need your four-wheel-drive vehicle to get there."

"I'll be there with coffee and Egg McMuffins to greet him. I don't mind driving. It's a rough ride, and I'm probably more familiar with it than anyone."

"Good. I'll send Mike Fletcher. He's one of the guys who originally worked on the barn scene. He'll have the vac, the generator, and everything you guys need to lay out a search grid. You might be able to wrap things up in one day, but I'll clear his schedule for as long as you need."

"Thanks Lester, looking forward to it."

"Good, I hope your day sucks tomorrow."

A WELCOME BREAK

IT WAS A GLORIOUS MONTH OF NO DRAMA for Trey, the Crafts, and Darell Metz. They were all beginning to think this year might turn out fine after all. Vicki appeared to be totally recovered physically, mentally, and emotionally. She hadn't spoken a word to anyone about going back to the Portal or about her plans. But she had plans.

She had spent the first week home from the hospital studying Dr. Jeffrey Long's case studies on near-death experiences while she planned another one of her own. She was thinking she would get stabbed this time. A string of Google searches settled her on "What kind of stomach stab wound would require surgery but not be life-threatening?" It turns out that if you can hit the liver or spleen, it may not be immediately life-threatening but should require exploratory surgery under anesthesia.

Vicki was going to order a box of books that she would be especially excited about, and while running to open the box with a large sharp knife, she would accidentally trip and fall, stabbing herself appropriately. She still had some details to work out, like the anatomy research to increase the likelihood of striking the intended targets as opposed to accidentally killing herself or wasting the effort on some superficial wound that wouldn't get her put to sleep. It also needed to be coordinated for a time when Trey, Michele, and Michael were all present to verify it was accidental and trigger immediate medical attention. She wasn't suicidal.

Abbey was right. These weren't good thoughts.

Vicki answered the Peacock Plume phone with a cheerful "Namaste."

"Vicki, I need your help," said Audrey.

Immediate panic and a startled response. "Elizabeth?"

Michael and Michele dropped what they were doing and looked at Vicki.

"What, oh no, gosh, I hadn't even thought about that for a month or more."

Vicki raised an open hand to Michael and Michele in an "all is well" gesture as she responded to Audrey, "I think about it all the time."

"I'm sorry I scared you. This is no emergency. Maybe I should be as alert, but things have been so peaceful and settled lately, I guess I've let my guard down."

Audrey took a deep breath and exhaled the tension. "I'm okay," she said with complete calm. "What's up."

"It's Lincoln."

"Kidnappers took Lincoln?" Vicki shouted, winking at Michael and Michele. "Just kidding, what can I do to be of service?"

"Richard and I are taking Elizabeth for her six months well-baby visit tomorrow. I messed up my calendar, and I also booked Lincoln for a grooming with Amy."

"Say no more, I'd love to spend a day with Lincoln and Amy. I haven't seen her since the wedding."

Amy was the flower girl at the joint Craft/Roadcap wedding last year. She worked at the animal shelter and was the one who initially put Lincoln and Richard together. She also had a part-time office at an animal hospital where she did pet grooming and helped with other services.

"Lincoln's appointment is at 10:00 a.m. We can drop him off to you on our way to the doctor's office."

"That works. See you in the a.m."

When Richard and Audrey showed up in the morning, Michele gushed, "How is the sweetest baby in the world and her little buddy Lincoln? Audrey, you really must plan some time away with Richard so I can house-sit these two again. That was an absolute pleasure for me."

"That's not a terrible idea," said Audrey. "A romantic getaway would be a treat. What do you think, Richard?"

"I don't hate it. Let's get Elizabeth and Lincoln through their scheduled maintenance visits first to see if we can afford it."

"Do it," said Vicki.

"Yes, do," added Michele. "I'd love to play mom again."

Richard said, "I won't rule it out, but we're running late for Elizabeth's checkup, so let's say I'm taking it under advisement."

"That means if we put it off, I may forget about it." Audrey laughed. "Okay, let's go, Romeo." She laughed again.

When they left, Vicki said, "That was a wonderful idea, Michele. Are you sure you wouldn't mind babysitting?"

"For Elizabeth? God no. I'd keep her forever if I could."

SERENDIPITY?

VICKI AND LINCOLN CHECKED IN AT THE front desk of the veterinary clinic. Lincoln was one of those unusual dogs that went happily to all doctors and groomers.

Amy greeted them with hugs. "How's my boy Lincoln?" she said, scratching him furiously while he bounced and barked his welcome. "Vicki, it's been forever since I saw you last. Audrey tells me you've had nothing but hospital trouble since the wedding. You look fine to me."

"For better or for worse, I'm back among the living. What have you been up to?"

"You might say I'm also back among the living. I have a boyfriend now, an Irish guy with the cutest accent. It was a long dry spell before that. I was horny and DTF every day with no takers."

"I seem to remember you even hit on Richard and Darell," Vicki said with a laugh.

"Before I found out that Darell has similar tastes in partners as we do," said Amy, joining the laughter. "Seriously, anything with a penis was on my radar for a long time."

"Where did you find your new flame?"

"Tinder, of all places. I was that desperate. He was my first hit. He looked hot, had a great résumé, and turned out not to be a creep, not that I would have cared about that at the time. We've been river dancing for months, and I may even be in love. His name is Danny O'Leary."

"Oh, Danny boy, the pipes, the pipes are calling ... " sang Vicki.

"You got that right. He's also got more than the average leprechaun and fills the pipes nicely."

"Good for you and Danny. Maybe I can be your flower girl this time."

"Fingers crossed. I do find my baby momma clock ticking lately. Come on, Lincoln, you're going to be my baby today. Walk this way," Amy said taking them to the lab she used as grooming quarters. "This is the hospital pharmacy and one of the pre-op prep rooms, but they let me use it when we're not busy. It has the metal table and big sinks and outlets for my vacuum blower and Dremel, so it works great for this."

"Pharmacy?" said Vicki, hearing a little bell tinkling.

"Yeah, that's also convenient. A lot of dogs need some sedation for grooming, but not my Lincoln, right, buddy!"

The bell got a little louder. "What do vets use for sedation?"

"The same stuff people use. Danny turned me on to try some of it out, and it's awesome good. I can't believe I've been around this stuff forever and never tried it. I've been throwing it away for years when it hits its expiration dates."

"I'd be scared I'd grow fur if I used doggie drugs."

"All you grow from this stuff is dreamy sex. I can hook you up if you want to give it a ride."

"Isn't it dangerous?"

"Not if you know what to do with it. You just do it a little at a time, and when you feel it starting to kick in, add a little more as you like. It's simple. I've probably tried it a dozen times now."

"Couldn't you get addicted?"

"Do I look like a drug addict?" Amy laughed. "It's not an opioid, and it's not even a controlled substance. People use it all the time for fun. How bad could it be?"

"You do make it sound interesting." Vicki hadn't said anything to Amy about the Portal; this could be her ticket back. "How much does one need to take?"

"Not much. Taking a look at you, I'd say 100 pounds."

"Holy shit!" gasped Vicki. "I don't know anything about it but that sounds like way too much."

Amy laughed louder. "Not 100 pounds of drugs, silly. I'm guessing your weight."

"Whew," Vicki recovered. "In that case, you're right on it."

"Then I already have a pre-mixed syringe with your name on it. Not your name actually, it says Shadow. Shadow was a 100-pound German Shepherd that was prepped for surgery yesterday but was put down instead."

"That's sad."

"Not really. Shadow had something called degenerative myelopathy, which causes weakness and paralysis starting in the back legs and progressing forward. He was already dragging his hind end and embarrassed by incontinence. It was only a matter of time before it moved to his lungs and killed him slowly. He also had a mast cell tumor that the surgery was scheduled for, but the family decided it was time to let him go. It was the right call."

"Still sad."

"But maybe not for you," Amy said as she handed Vicki a syringe marked "Shadow PropoFlo."

"Huh, PropoFlo. I know I had propofol in the hospital, what is this?"

"It's the same thing. When they package it for veterinary clinics, they add a preservative to extend the shelf life since it gets used in smaller quantities than in a people hospital. We're supposed to dispose of it 28 days after opening, but I've tried some that was months old and it still does the same thing. Try it, I promise you'll like it."

"I could never tell Trey about this."

"Believe me, neither one of us will ever tell anyone about this. It's just between us girls."

"Well, we'll see," said Vicki putting the syringe in a pocket of her purse. She heard one last soft tinkle of her bell as she thought, *"Now I have the ways, I just need to find the means."*

"Okay, Lincoln," announced Amy. "Let's get you started. Furminator first, into the tub, and on to your manicure. You'll be spanking new and reeking of Giorgio Armani in an hour or so."

The well-baby visit was perfect, pronouncing Elizabeth both healthy and quite advanced in development for her age. Vicki dropped off the stinky Lincoln to cuddle with the exceptional Elizabeth and moved on to her new project.

GOING BACK

VICKI LOVED THE NEW PLAN. SHE WOULDN'T have to stab herself after all. She had turned her Google searches to something new and finally hit on the perfect solution. "What symptoms would get a patient on heart and lung monitors at an emergency room?" gave her the AI-assisted response she was looking for:

"Patients experiencing severe chest pain, shortness of breath, nausea, and other symptoms that could indicate a heart attack or lung condition would typically be placed on heart and lung monitors at the emergency room. These monitors are essential for monitoring vital signs and ensuring immediate medical intervention if necessary."

Problem solved!

She had the drugs to take her where she needed to go, and she now had the means to self-administer the solution in a medically controlled environment. All she had to do was check into the ER with the right complaints. No danger, no concerns, and no time like the present.

The timing was perfect. Trey was off with Richard visiting contractors for the next steps in the Peacock Plume building renovation. Scope creep had taken their project beyond parking lot paving to new windows, new floors, and a total repaint of the exterior. Sometime in the near future the shop will be shutting down for weeks for a complete refreshment and a grand reopening.

Vicki told Michele and Michael that she had some errands to run. The Portal was beckoning as she headed back to the now very familiar hospital.

She made sure to shuffle slowly from the parking lot to the ER with a grimace on her face in case she was on camera. "Yes, ma'am," she was greeted at the check-in desk.

With her pained look and clutching her chest, she said weakly, "I was driving by when I suddenly had chest pain and it's hard to breathe. Please, I think I may have to throw up."

That was the end of check-in. Two attendants rapidly appeared with a wheelchair and whisked her past the big doors into one of the emergency room bays. "What is your pain level now?" asked one.

"It seems to be getting a little better," she said softly. "It was a ten in the car but probably a three right now."

Vicki convinced the male attendants she could change to a hospital gown on her own.

"We'll give you some privacy. We're right on the other side of the curtain."

She had dressed only in sweats for this drive so she could change quickly. Before she gave an all-clear signal, she retrieved the syringe and carefully tucked it between her butt cheeks as she settled onto the bed, *"This would be a bad time for a case of premature inoculation."* She thought chuckling to herself.

"Okay," she said softly. "The pain is coming back."

A female attendant had now joined the team, attaching electrode pads to her chest, stringing wires, and covering her back up. The others were rapidly setting up an array of equipment.

"We're getting you connected for a quick EKG, and you'll stay on the heart monitor while you're here."

"Box One checked!"

"This IV line," she said, poking a needle into the back of Vicki's left hand, "will let us give you some fluids and give us a port to administer any other injections so we don't have to keep poking you. I also need to take a blood sample for the lab, and I can get that from here."

"Ooh, I get my own port, this is really going well."

They wrapped a small tube around her head with nostril probes to give her oxygen and clipped a blood ox sensor to her right index finger. "This will allow us to keep on top of any changes in your oxygen levels."

"Box Two checked, that should do it."

"Tell me your pain level right now."

"About a six or seven," Vicki croaked.

"Do you have any medical history of heart disease?"

"No."

"Any other health problems?"

"No."

"Do you smoke, drink, or use recreational drugs?"

"An occasional glass of wine, but nothing else."

"Do you currently take any medicines, either prescription or over the counter?"

"No."

"Any dietary or herbal supplements?"

"A daily multi-vitamin. Does that count?"

"No problem. Those are all the best answers. I'm starting an IV with some fluids. It also delivers aspirin and nitroglycerine, which may start bringing some relief for your pain. Any nausea currently?"

"No, thankfully."

"All good news. Do you think you can rest now that we've poked and prodded and punctured and wired you up?"

"I am feeling much better."

"Good, we need just a little time to run your blood test and go over the EKG. You have a call button at your right hand. Don't be shy about using it for anything, even just a drink of water. Try to relax, and I'll be back with one of the physicians as soon as we have your results."

"Thank you."

"It's what we do," said the attendant as she pulled the curtain closed behind her. The others had already left, and Vicki was alone.

"I should get an Academy Award for this performance," she thought as she retrieved the syringe from its hiding place.

She pulled the cap off the needle. Tapping the syringe and giving it a little squirt like she'd seen on the doctor shows, she poked it into the port on the IV connection and gave herself a small injection from the plunger. And waited. In less than a minute she knew it was the right stuff. *"Amy said a little at a time."*

Vicki pushed in a second small dose. She was waiting again when the female tech returned and the curtain pulled back. Panic! She tried to hide her hands with the blanket, but the woman had already seen the syringe.

"What are you doing?" she shouted, surprised and alarmed.

Vicki pushed the plunger all the way in. Pleading with her eyes to the woman who was pulling the syringe from the port, Vicki was gone in seconds.

THE HUNT FOR ISABEL

ABBEY FOSTER JOINED DON WESTON AT HIS office around 6:30 for coffee. When Mike Fletcher arrived from Harrisburg they made quick introductions over Egg McMuffins, loaded Don's cruiser, and headed off on the rocky journey to Glenn Weaver's hundred-acre woods. All seemed undisturbed as Don removed the crime scene tape from the rutted lane and drove all the way to the site.

Don showed Mike and Abbey the particles he had found on his last trip. The three prospectors surveyed the scene of the Stonehenge field, using small rakes to sift through the thatch of the heavy grass and surface the hiding spots of more granules.

"Okay," announced Mike. "I think we've got our search area. It seems to be confined to the circle of the foam rocks. I'll get the stakes and the string so we can mark grid lines for our search lanes."

When the marking was done, Mike gave further instructions. "You two start at Zone One with some aggressive raking to break up the ground cover. We should be able to surface more of our target evidence at the dirt level. It will take me a few minutes to set up the generator and vacuum. I'll follow you through the grid, and we'll capture whatever we can of the clay fragments we find there."

"What are your thoughts on the DNA value of what we collect?" asked Don.

"I think the potential is good enough that a sizable sample will be more than sufficient. We can go through the whole area and try to gather everything if you'd like to, but that may not be necessary."

"What do you consider a sizable sample?"

"A cup of the granules would be more than enough for testing, but I'd target a quart for good measure. If it is absorbent material, as it appears to be, and it was used to collect blood and body pieces, the DNA will be throughout."

"In that case, what do you think about starting in the middle? It might yield more than the fringes."

"That's a good suggestion. We have everything mapped up so we won't miss any spot, but we may find what we need pretty quickly by targeting the center. Let's do that. Pick your raking spots, and I'll follow."

It was a good suggestion. In less than two hours they had a full quart of the grains.

"Should we continue?" asked Abbey. "I'm used to archeology digs where we turn over every stone and sift every grain of dirt."

"Nothing prevents us from returning, if need be," said Mike. "But I'm confident we already have much more than we need to process it for evidence. I'm here for whatever the two of you want to do, but I'd vote to get this sample to the lab. We'll know in three days' time if our victim is a part of it."

"Good enough," said Don. "Let's call it a wrap and see what we've found."

THE AWAKENING

VICKI WAS IN A FOG BUT NOT IN THE PORTAL as she heard a familiar voice. It was Dr. Cole saying, "Administer the rocuronium in case we need to intubate."

She kept her eyes closed. *"If Dr. Cole is here, I must be in trouble,"* she thought, overcome by an immense guilt.

"Vicki, Vicki, Vicki," he said out loud to himself. "What have you done."

The female attendant confirmed a drop in respiratory rate and blood pressure. "Should we intubate?"

"Not yet. If it is a propofol product as labeled, the effects should diminish rapidly. Barring seizure or arrest, she shouldn't need additional intervention. If we don't see reversal of those numbers in the next fifteen minutes, we'll reassess."

Vicki was scared. *"It didn't work, I can't get the answers, I shouldn't have tried this, what will Trey and Audrey think, I've let down the doctors and all my friends, what will happen now?"* So many thoughts raced through her mind as she stayed hidden behind her eyelids, afraid to show she was awake.

In less than ten minutes her oxygen levels and blood pressure were returning to normal ranges.

"Emergency over," pronounced Dr. Cole to the attendants. "You can record in your log that I accepted responsibility for the next phase of patient care. You can also have your treatment bay back for the next person who needs it. I'll have Dr. Justice send transport for her admission to the psych ward."

"Psych ward? Dr. Justice? Please God take me to the Portal and let me never wake up."

PSYCH

TWENTY MINUTES LATER VICKI WAS IN A hospital room, just her and Dr. Cole. "You can open your eyes and talk now," he said as he removed the ratchet strap across her pelvis and her wrist restraints. "I know you're in there. You need to give some answers so I can clear you medically and we can get the proper help for you."

"I'm so sorry," she said.

"I shouldn't have to be here," he said. "One of the ER nurses recognized your name and let me know you were having a cardiac event. I left the bedside of a child with a gunshot wound to find you in distress over a seemingly selfish pursuit of something we had talked about and warned you against."

"I was trying to be responsible."

"You are responsible," he continued. "For needlessly tying up emergency resources for something that never should have happened. Did you really have cardiac symptoms when you came here today?"

"No, I just wanted to make sure I'd have the proper medical monitoring you told me about for the safe use of propofol. I didn't want anything to go wrong."

"So, you had no real medical conditions of concern, and what I witnessed was only caused by propofol toxicity from your unqualified and ignorant self-injection?"

"I guess," she said, crying now.

"Well, something went very wrong, didn't it?" he paused as she sobbed. Softening a bit, he said, "Based on this conversation, if I can trust what you tell me, your immediate medical concerns are now passed. Your mental health concerns are just beginning. We can help you with those here, but you'll have to be completely honest with us."

"I'll never lie to you again," she said, whimpering. "What happens now? Does Trey need to know about this?"

"He does."

"He'll never trust me again."

Dr. Cole made the complete shift to bedside manners. "He will." Taking her hand. "He will, we're going to take steps to fix this, starting now. Tom, are you there?"

Dr. Justice entered the room. "I was looking forward to seeing you again," he said to Vicki. "I'm sorry it had to be like this."

Vicki broke down and bawled, "It didn't have to be. It's all my fault that I let everyone down."

"That understanding and admission is a start," he spoke. "With your permission I'd like to get you some food and rest for today while I visit with Trey and your friends. There are some legal issues connected with your actions today that I need to consider before we move on to treatment."

"I give up. You've both been so good to me, and I've been so selfish. I just wanted to help Elizabeth. I'll do whatever you think is right." Tears falling.

"I think the right thing is to simply relax and rest as much as possible today. I'll give you something to help with that. While you're here, I want you to think of this room as a hotel rather than a hospital. You have full access to room service, reading materials, whatever you want that will make your stay as normal as possible. Promise me you'll be okay for today while I set up our next steps."

"I promise I'm not thinking of suicide or any other stupid acts. I'm only thinking of how foolish I've been and hoping you can make things better."

"Good, then Dr. Cole and I will move on to our respective duties. I'll check in this evening to start our next steps."

"Dr. Cole," Vicki said. "I'm sorry that I wasted everyone's time and took you away from something more important."

"No matter now, I got the text about twenty minutes ago that the boy didn't make it."

NEXT STEPS

TREY WAS BACK AT THE PEACOCK PLUME taking window measurements with Michael when the phone rang.

"Namaste," answered Michele. She listened briefly and called out, "Trey, it's for you, one of the doctors from Virginia Hospital Center."

He took the phone, "This is Trey."

"Trey, Dr. Tom Justice here. We met about a month ago when your wife was in the hospital."

"I remember."

"'I want you to know that Vicki's healthy, but she's here in the hospital again. I wonder if you can come over and visit with me?"

"What's going on?"

Dr. Justice filled him in on the details of the day and why he felt it was best for Vicki to stay over. "I would encourage you to work with me to stage an intervention so we can get Vicki the help I believe she needs."

"I'm listening."

"There are some legal concerns stemming from her actions. Her choices unquestionably meet the qualification of a subject causing serious physical harm to themselves. That is something that should be reported to authorities. The result of that would be an Involuntary Custody Order and confinement to the Arlington Community Services Board for clinical evaluation. We can avoid that if she voluntarily submits to stay under our care here for that evaluation. I believe she's ready to do that, but I'd like to initiate that with a family intervention to help her decide."

"Tell me how that works."

"I'd need to meet with you and any other family to prepare everyone. We need to get out in the open any frustrations or anger that her actions are causing in those close to her."

"Her fascination with the occult stuff has always intrigued and amused me, but since the accident it's become an overwhelming obsession. I'm afraid I'm going to lose her, and I don't know what to do."

"That is what she needs to hear from you and those she loves to help her think differently and make better decisions. The best time to do this is now when she's still feeling guilty and uncertain. How quickly do you think we could get the family together?"

"There is no genetic family, but there are several close friends that she and I certainly consider family, especially her partner Audrey. They'll all be as crushed as I am to hear what happened today, and they will all drop anything to help her. I can start making phone calls and get back to you. Is this number on the caller ID your best contact?"

"Yes, that's my cell."

"I'll call you shortly."

"I'll make necessary arrangements here at the hospital. Thank you."

Trey put the phone down, looking at a wide-eyed Michael and Michele. "I take it you heard all of that?"

"What can we do to help?" asked Michele.

"If I can round up Audrey and Richard to come to the hospital with me, would you be able to stay with Elizabeth?"

"I'd do anything for Elizabeth, you know that."

"Good, that's the first step. I'm going upstairs to change and make a couple of calls."

"We love you and Vicki," Michele said as Trey walked off.

The Craft house was the first call. "Richard, it's Trey, is Audrey there?"

"Right here. We're all hanging out by the fire."

"Good, put me on speaker phone. Vicki is in the hospital again."

Trey went over the conversation with Dr. Justice and let them know he had already asked Michele about staying with Elizabeth. "I can bring her over and pick you up in half an hour if you can do this."

"Then we're ready to go," said Audrey.

The call to Darell was next. "Where did she get the drugs?" was his first question.

"I don't know. I don't know a lot, but I know your voice will be important to her if you can join us. I'm picking up Richard and Audrey as soon as I get off the phone with you. Do you want to meet us at their place?"

"No. I'll meet you at the hospital. I need to do some quick research. I'll see you there in an hour."

Trey let the doctor know they'd all be there in an hour.

INTERVENTION

DR. JUSTICE MET THEM AT THE HOSPITAL entrance. Darell arrived as Trey was making introductions.

"I've arranged a conference room for us. I'd like to make sure we're all on the same page when I bring Vicki in."

On the elevator, Darell asked, "Do you know where she got the drugs?"

"I don't. That part will fall into your jurisdiction once we get her voluntary consent for clinical evaluation. Our only concern was her physical condition and state of mind. I'd say both of those are currently stable. She has a lot of guilt and remorse right now. The four of you have an important part in her next steps."

Once they were settled in the conference room, the doctor started with, "I've already explained to Trey the legal position we need to address, Technically, Vicki is still being held under medical care for her emergency room event, but the reasonable limits of that are probably close to an end, at which time she and Trey could decide to leave. If that would be their decision, I would be forced to invoke an Emergency Custody Order."

"I would agree with that," said Darell. "She has clearly demonstrated a substantial likelihood of causing serious physical harm to herself."

The others looked at Darell and the doctor. "What would happen to her?" asked Audrey.

"She would be removed from our care and placed with the Community Services Board for clinical evaluation," said Dr. Justice. "I'd prefer not to go that route. Her transfer would also require disclosure to the board of all medical records. An independent reviewer would have eight hours to process the circumstances of her hospitalization and all physician notes. With no other background, a cold read of her record is likely to be judged as a presently suicidal patient with a record of mental confusion and hallucinations. We know Vicki here, and I know we can help her."

"She has to stay here," said Trey.

"That will be up to you and Vicki to consent to a voluntary program of further analysis and treatment in my care. I don't anticipate strong resistance from her. She is ashamed of her behavior and aware that it is hurtful to those that love and trust her. She doesn't know you are here. When I bring her in, I'd like Trey to talk first."

"What should I say?" he asked.

"She should expect anger and frustration, and you should certainly have both of those, but what we are about to do for Vicki is not confrontation or interrogation. It's an opportunity for each participant to address her, acknowledging how her choices have hurt you but expressing your willingness to help her get beyond what is causing her to make such choices. Let her know you love her and you're glad that she is okay physically. Then acknowledge your pain and close with support. Your statements should be brief but direct on those points. I'll moderate as needed and not allow her to talk until we've gone around the table, one by one, and given her our thoughts. Are we ready?" Heads nodded.

Vicki was surprised and visibly affected when she entered the room. Her expression reflected astonishment, curiosity, and fear all at once. "What are you all doing here?" she asked tentatively.

"They all wanted to see you," said Tom as he guided her to a chair next to Trey.

Trey took her hand and started. "Vicki, I love you more than anything in life. You're my angel, my dreams, my future, and I'm blessed that you're my wife. But I feel I'm losing you. I love your quirky supernatural sense, but I'm afraid that obsession has become more important to you than our life together, and I can't accept that. I need us to go back to being us. I need to know if you want that too. I can't go on with you if I live in fear of your death because I can't go on without you in my life. Please come back from whatever it is that is calling you away from me. I know you can do it and I want to help. I will always love you."

Vicki was crying now. "I want ..."

The doctor interrupted as he set a box of Kleenex in front of her. "Vicki, Trey has expressed some genuine love and concern. Let's hear out the rest of the group before we talk."

Richard and Darell went next in line. Their testimonies followed the same message of love and the same sadness of loss.

Audrey was last. "Vicki you're the sister I never had. We've been through so much in our lives together. We've laughed, we cried and grieved, and we've always been there for each other. And now Elizabeth needs you too. We girls need to stick together. I know what you did today was for her, but you see it didn't help at all. It frightened all of us. We need you, I need you, to stop the path you're on. I'll be with you through every step to help you do that. We'll find the best way, but this isn't it. Tell me you still love me and all of us. We want to have you in our lives forever."

"Vicki?" said the doctor.

The tears had never stopped from the beginning. It took her almost a minute to compose herself enough to speak. She wiped her wet eyes and face. Her words came haltingly.

"I love every one of you. You goofballs are the only real family I've ever had. Trey, without you in my life, I'd be just another cat lady playing with her crystals. You've brought me into a real world beyond my occult curiosities and a real love I never knew could be. Audrey, you adopted me when no one else would. I knew sisterhood and a spiritual connection the moment I met you. Then you brought Richard, the biggest goofball, and Darell. And they may not know it yet, but I'm sure I've also disappointed Don and Abbey, and I'll have to face that too.

"All of you have given me friendship and love, and I've brought you pain by being a pain. I know I've been given a gift to sense some things that others can't. I know Audrey and Abbey and even Elizabeth share that gift, but I've made it a selfish addiction and turned the potential of powerful good to pain for people I love and need. I'm so sorry," she said, breaking down completely.

Trey swept her up in a hug that was joined by the others with tears and murmurs of "I love you," and "it's okay," and "everything will be good again."

Tom let them stay that way for some time before he spoke. "I hate to break this up, but Vicki, in fairness to your patient's rights, time is running out on a decision that needs to be made."

"I'm ready to go home now," Vicki said quietly, sniffling and wiping her tears.

"I'm afraid that, based on your actions today, I can't let you do that. My suggestion is that you should make a conscious and voluntary choice to stay here in my care. If you don't make that choice, I'll have to ask your friend Darell to take charge of you under an Emergency Custody Order."

She looked at Darell. "What does that mean?"

"Vicki, you need to agree to stay here for now. Under an Emergency Custody Order, I would be required to transport you to a public mental health facility for evaluation. You don't want that. Dr. Justice knows you and has only your best interests in mind. If I take you from here, you'll end up in a cell surrounded by strangers."

"I can't go home?" she said sadly.

"You demonstrated a willingness to cause harm to yourself by your actions today. That can't be ignored, legally or medically. If you don't choose to stay here willingly, you will be moved to the custody of the Community Services Board to decide your future."

"Trey?"

"You need to agree to stay here for now. If you love me and you want this to get better, you'll agree to that."

"Audrey? Richard?"

"We all agree," said Audrey. "Staying here for now is the only right choice you have for all of us. Please say yes."

After a long silence and more tears, Vicki consented.

GOOD MORNING

TOM JUSTICE RAPPED LIGHTLY ON VICKI'S door before entering. He brought coffee and a continental breakfast on a tray. "I saw you hadn't called room service, so I thought you may be getting hungry."

"I do like the cinnamon buns here."

"I hope you found your first night's accommodations at Hotel Hospital satisfactory."

"They forgot the mint on the pillow. Can you do something about that?"

"I'll work on it. I'm glad to see you haven't loss your sense of humor."

"From what Darell said last night, my only option came with iron bars and soap on a rope. This is marginally better. When can I go home?"

"Soon, I hope. That depends on our progress. Starting this afternoon, you and I will have two meeting times each day, morning and afternoon. The rest of the day is yours. While you can't leave the ward, you are free to roam as you choose, so don't feel like you're trapped in this room. There are several open common areas always available to you, including an out-door sun deck, a kitchen, and a small library. You can keep your phone, and you have full internet access. You're welcome to have guests at any time. There are two already waiting to see you as soon as I get out of here. Any questions?"

"Where is the pool?"

"I'll check on that when I arrange for your mint. Seriously, I want you to make yourself at home as best you can. The fact that you aren't seeming anxious or depressed and you have a sense of humor is a great start to our work together, which will commence today. There is a notebook on your desk. Use it. Journaling will be daily homework. I'll see you at 2:00 p.m. in my office."

"Thank you."

"Thank you for choosing Hotel Hospital for your vacation."

"Next," he said as he departed and Darell and Trey came in. Darell was holding the stuffed sheltie.

"You brought faux Lincoln back. Does that mean you're going to try to make me laugh again?"

"Try being the operative word," said Trey as he kissed Vicki on the cheek. "How are you doing?"

"Still embarrassed and ashamed and missing you."

"I miss you too. Do what you need to do here, and you'll be home sooner than you think."

"Then I'll make love to you three times a day."

"You're not supposed to lie to us, so I'll have Darell make that statement an official part of the police report."

Vicki's eyes opened wide. "Darell, is there a police report?"

"No, but there would have been if you hadn't volunteered to stay here."

"Really?"

"Really. Putting you under a protective custody order would have required it. You dodged several bullets by making the right choice. That was just the first one."

"Okay, but you're not making me laugh."

"It's not a laughing matter."

"Sorry."

"Me too. Can you tell me where you got the syringe of drugs? I think I know but I want to hear it from you."

Long pause.

"This is all my fault. I don't want to get anyone in trouble."

"Someone created their own trouble when they gave that to you. I'm going to have a talk with them about the consequences. Right now, I'm able to be here as a friend. I spent last night doing research on potential criminal charges and penalties related to what happened yesterday. Those start with possession. Both you and the supplier could be guilty of that. Then there is distribution, and, in the case of a health care professional, unprofessional conduct and violation of licensing regulations. If you tell me who gave you that, I may be able to stay a friend to help them as well."

"You said you think you know who it was. Who do you think?"

"Based on the labeling, my guess is Amy. Did I guess right?"

"Yes," quietly. "But she didn't mean any harm by it."

"Friends giving drugs to friends rarely do, but I see damage and death all the time because of it. Had you died, homicide charges would have been added to the list.

"Bullet Number Two avoided is that you didn't choose ketamine, and the current state of the law on propofol is vague. Federal law does not classify propofol as a controlled substance, and Virginia law defaults to that definition. States can add their own definitions of controlled substances. The ketamine you asked me about has that designation in Virginia. Possession and/or distribution of a controlled substance is a felony subject to significant fines and many years in prison.

"Bullet Three avoided is timing. There is a current bill moving through the legislature that will add propofol to that list. Today, however, it is seen in the eyes of the law as a non-narcotic Category VI drug, a Class 4 misdemeanor punishable by a $250 fine and less than twelve months imprisonment. A first-time offender will typically be admitted to a drug diversion program with charges dismissed upon successful completion."

"Does that mean Amy is not in big trouble?"

"Does she use this drug herself?"

"Only recently. Her new boyfriend introduced her to it."

"Then I'd say they're both in big trouble. Maybe not in a current legal sense but certainly by thinking they can use these types of drugs for fun and recreation. She needs to start making better choices. I'd like to help her as a friend, but having Arlington County Police Sergeant Darell Metz pay her a visit may be more productive."

FIRST SESSION

AT 2:00 P.M. VICKI WANDERED INTO THE office of Dr. Tom Justice. Dr. Cole was with him.

"Are you guys still mad at me?"

"Let's leave it at disappointed," said Dr. Cole. "But I understand the two of you will fix that starting today. I'm happy to see you up and healthy."

"Thanks, are you here because of me?"

"Not this time. Tom was filling me in on all the studies and breakthroughs from his month of international conferences, you know, the sightseeing and wine tours. I may have to build a scientific sabbatical into my own schedule next year. There's so much to learn," he said with a wry smile. "Well, you two have some real business to discuss, so I'll see myself out."

"Wait, Dr. Cole," said Vicki. "I have a question."

"Shoot."

"When I took the propofol yesterday, why didn't I go back to the Portal? Did I do something wrong?"

"Let's first agree that in the realm of common sense and sensible adult behavior, yes, you did something very wrong."

"I won't fight you on that, but I had to get the answer from there to save Elizabeth. Why couldn't I do that? Elizabeth would be protected now, and I wouldn't have to be here."

"Hmmmm ... maybe I should be mad at you. Don't fight me on this either. The minute you walked into that ER faking cardiac symptoms, you were unquestionably going to end up right where you are now."

"But I did that to make it safe, so I'd already be medically monitored while I took it."

"Being medically monitored through anesthetic use of propofol means under the care of a skilled anesthesiologist controlling the successive small doses of the drug to put you under and keep you in a sedated state. What you did was like jumping through a window without opening it first." Dr. Cole continued in a raised voice of frustration, "If you had a larger dose in that syringe, you wouldn't have to be here, and you would have made it to the Portal but only because you would be dead."

Quiet.

"I'm sorry. I am glad to see you physically well, and I look forward to the time soon when you are completely well and understand that only God should be playing God. You two have some work to do, and I'm in the way of that. Press on," he said as he left.

Quiet.

"The answer is in the Portal, and I can't get there," said Vicki, almost in a whisper. "I'm not sure how I should feel right now."

"Confused, probably hurt, maybe convicted. He is speaking his genuine truth. He's also hurt. He does care about your well-being, you know."

"I think so. I guess I must be honest with you about everything?"

"We won't make progress if you're not."

"Then you should know why I thought I was being responsible by using the drugs." She told Dr. Justice about her previous thoughts on getting under anesthesia by stabbing herself.

"I'm glad you shared that with me. It confirms that you're in the right place now and hopefully in the right state of mind to reconsider what got you here. Are you ready to get to work?"

"It sounds like I'd better be."

"I think you are. Let's start walking through your life. Some time ago we left off with Mrs. Monahan introducing you to what we might call a paranormal awakening before her untimely death. How did you find your way from there to the Peacock Plume?"

Vicki was still a little stunned by Dr. Cole's comments. She took some deep breaths to compose herself and thought about Mrs. Monahan's warning of testing the gift carefully. Maybe she had been trying to play God.

After about thirty seconds she started slowly: "I remember that I started spending all my time at the big library reading everything they had on people like me. That's where I discovered the American Society for Psychical Research, which seemed to confirm I was not alone. They did regular programs with speakers at their headquarters, but that was in New York, which was out of reach for me at the time, so I looked for local connections at the places with signs for tarot and palm readings."

"Did you find your people there?"

"Not really. I did get pretty good at recognizing false promises and predictions from bad magicians and fakes. That sent me deeper into the library collections and a focus on the power and beauty of crystals, which led the path to the Peacock Plume. I learned to take my little bag and shovel to local creeks, riverbeds, and hillsides where the crystals could be found in nature. I started showing and selling them at local flea markets. That raised enough money to start buying the types of crystals I couldn't gather on my own. The library had gotten pretty used to me by then and allowed me a monthly space to show my collection and share what I had learned."

"Where were you living then?"

"Through junior and senior high school, my foster care was a group home. An older retired Christian couple took in eight to twelve of us unwanted older orphans and runaways at a time. It was a strict conservative house with daily Bible readings. They had a calling to save us before the system would turn is out into the world of sin." Vicki laughed. She was beginning to get more comfortable in her conversation with Dr. Justice.

"Do I sense some rebellion?" Tom laughed with her.

"Most of the kids who came through there were short-timers and ran away again when they figured out what they had gotten into. But there was a core group that went through the motions to appease their mission in exchange for a safe house and relative freedom away from there. I don't know if I was saved or not by the experience, but I was okay with the spiritual aspect, so I flew under the radar of hell and brimstone."

"So, you started building an audience of future customers through the entrepreneurial outreach of the flea markets and library shows?"

"Some I still see today."

"How old were you at that time?"

"Seventeen and I looked like I was twelve."

"But people came to see what you had to offer?"

"Quite a few. I had done my homework. When I was released from the foster care system, I found a cheap storefront to rent in a run-down strip mall. That's where I met Audrey. She had an art gallery in the same mall. We were one-man shows trying to survive."

"Dr. Cole told me about Audrey when you and I first met. He said the two of you were like sisters. I saw that in her words to you yesterday."

"Closer than that. She was the first person in my life that I knew had the same gift. She doesn't see it, but she has it."

"Where did you live then?"

"Most nights I slept in the store, sometimes on the street."

"That must have been a hard time."

"Not really. I learned a lot of survival skills from the early years with my mom. I knew where the barber college was where you could get a haircut for a couple of dollars, I knew where to get clothes for free, and I wasn't above dumpster diving for food." She giggled.

"Wow."

"I can still tell you where there's a Pizza Hut that throws out whole pizzas every night still in the box."

"How did you and Audrey get from the strip mall to the Peacock Plume?"

"We shared our lunches every day. She had a skeptical curiosity about the crystals and the paranormal, and I was fascinated by her art. I can barely draw a stick figure, and she makes real life happen with a brush and some paint, or even a pencil. I knew in my heart and my dreams that we would always be connected. I think she did too. Then one day the opportunity to think about a business together was dropped in our laps."

"How so?"

"One of my customers was a realtor and told me about an old building she thought would be perfect for my shop. Audrey came with me to look at it. It needed a lot of TLC, but it felt right. There was plenty of space for my shop and her gallery and an apartment upstairs where we could live. With no more housing expenses and no more shop leases, it seemed doable. Neither of us had much in savings, but we had enough credibility established in our little businesses to qualify for a loan, so we took the leap and bought the place as partners."

"Okay, we made it through overcoming adolescence and adversity to the beginning of the Peacock Plume. Challenging but hopeful times. We'll pick you up there tomorrow with more Audrey and how you met Trey. This is a good place to stop for the day. How are you feeling?"

"A little better. Do you agree with Dr. Cole? Was I that close to losing Trey and Audrey forever?"

"Yes."

SHE DOES EXIST

AUDREY CALLED ABBEY FOSTER.

"I have news about Vicki, but first I owe you an apology for being mean to you. I hope you can forgive me."

"I'm so glad you called. There's nothing to forgive on my end. I'm the one that needs forgiveness for my negligence."

"Isabel told Audrey that no harm was done. I overreacted and blamed you."

"You were only doing what a mother should do to protect her daughter. Let's just agree that neither of us were at our best in the emotions of that time. Our friendship is more important than anything that happened that day."

"Agreed."

"What's the news about Vicki?"

"She's in the hospital again. She almost killed herself trying to get back to Isabel." Audrey told Abbey all the details from the ER to the psych ward. "We need to stay close to her and convince her to give up on the Portal. It's too dangerous."

"I'll let Don know what's going on. And I have news for you. Isabel may be coming back to us without the Portal. Don and I worked with someone from the state forensics office to gather pieces of the stuff that may have been used to dispose of her body. It was all over the Stonehenge field just like Isabel said it should be. They think it's possible her DNA is still there. They have a lab testing it now. They got it Monday night so you should get a call from Don Thursday morning with a yea or nay."

"Trey and Darell have been visiting with Vicki in the mornings, but I'll switch with them for Thursday. Tell him to call on Vicki's phone. I won't say anything to her until we hear from Don."

"You said she's in a psych ward. Is she going to be okay?"

"Yes, for sure. Her primary doctor now is someone who is very sympathetic to her paranormal path. He interviewed her during the last hospital stay, and they were going to do some journal articles together on near-death experience. If you and Don have found Isabel from Vicki's Portal revelation, he'll have to agree she's not crazy or suicidal, she's gifted and stupid."

DAY TWO
IN THE WARD

DARELL AND TREY WERE THE EARLY VISI-
tors again the next morning. They brought coffee and a breakfast tray from the kitchen.

"How did Day One go?" asked Trey.

Vicki pushed out her lower lip in an exaggerated pout. "Dr.
Cole yelled at me."

Darell laughed out loud, "Good for him. I can't imagine the
good Dr. Cole yelling, but someone needed to."

"Did you deserve it?" asked Trey.

"He basically said I was stupid and almost killed myself. Dr.
Justice agreed, so, yeah, I guess I deserved it."

"Aside from that, Mrs. Lincoln, how did you enjoy the play?"
said Darell, still smiling.

"Funny guy."

"Seriously, what did you and Dr. Justice talk about?"

"We went back to my childhood. He was interested in how I
grew up, how I found out I was different than others, and how
I got to the Peacock Plume. I think we're going to talk more
about Audrey today."

"What made him think you grew up?"

"Trey, would you punch him please?"

"I would, but he's got a gun."

"I'm glad you two are enjoying yourselves while I'm locked up here," she said sarcastically.

"I wouldn't mind being locked up here," said Trey. "These cinnamon buns are like crack. If you'll excuse me, I'm going back for more."

"There's no excuse for you," she said. "But bring me some more coffee while you're up."

When Trey left, Darell got serious. "I visited Amy yesterday. She was surprised when I told her what happened to you and what my thoughts were about her role."

"What will happen to her now?"

"That ball's in her court. She was genuinely scared and remorseful. I gave her the contact for an outpatient substance abuse resource. I'm going to check today to see that she made the call and scheduled an assessment. I don't think Amy is an addict, but she has a lot to learn about her choices to avoid becoming one. She knows she can still be charged for possession and distribution in your case. She also knows I'd prefer not to do that, as it would implicate you as well."

"Do you think she'll do what you said?"

"I do. Things could get messy for both of you if she doesn't. You might want to give her a call."

"I'll do that."

Trey returned with more coffee. "God these things are good," he said muffled by the cinnamon bun in his mouth. He was on his third one.

"You better knock that off. If I ever get out of here, I'm going to be horny as hell, and a slow fat guy just isn't going to do it for me."

"Now I'm conflicted," he said. "Making love three times a day is certainly attractive, but losing the connection for these cinnamon buns … what's a boy to do."

"You can put butter and cinnamon on my buns if you get me out of here."

"Then get well soon. I like that idea."

"I do too," she said with a throaty laugh. "You boys run along and play now. I have a 10:00 with Dr. Justice, and I'm now highly motivated to convince him I should be at home."

The morning session went well. Tom had some commentary to keep things on track every now and then, but mostly Vicki just talked. Her relationship with Audrey began her adult life. That and meeting Trey helped her bring her paranormal into the normal world.

There were sad chapters like the death of Audrey's fiancé, but they all overcame the obstacles that life put out there and grew stronger together. When Audrey met Richard and got pulled into the puzzle of his haunted house, they also met Darell and Don and Abbey, and of course Lincoln. Now the Crafts and the Roadcaps were married and Elizabeth had arrived to add to the family.

Vicki got a little emotional at that point. "I thought I was doing the best thing for Elizabeth, but I almost lost her and everyone else too."

"You might write that in your journal. It's a good recognition to hold on to. That will wrap up our morning. We'll meet again at 2:00."

"Thanks."

When Vicki got back to her room, she called Amy.

"Oh Vicki, I'm so sorry, but I can't talk right now. Can I call you back in an hour?"

"Sure."

"*That's odd,*" thought Vicki. She stretched out on the bed, wrote some things in her journal, and closed her eyes. She was tired.

Vicki saw the Portal in a dream. Something that could be Isabel's shape was a blurry haze on the other side. She stood at the entrance. It was like a rubber wall closed it off. She could push her hand into it but not through it. She woke to the ringing vibrating phone on her chest. It was Amy. Ninety minutes had passed since Vicki called her.

"Vicki, are you okay? Darell came to see me at the vet's office yesterday."

"I know."

"He told me what happened. I'm an idiot."

"I'm the idiot. You couldn't have known what I was going to do with that stuff. It's my fault, not yours."

"I think he wanted to arrest me. He probably should have for what I did to you."

"You didn't do anything to me. I did it to myself. I never told him you gave it to me. He figured it out somehow from the syringe. What did he say to you?"

"That I don't know what I'm messing with. He gave me a number for a clinic and told me if I didn't get help now it was only a matter of time before I'd be in jail or dead. He scared me."

"Have you called them?"

"I went there in person. That's why I couldn't talk when you called earlier. I was just going in to see a counselor there."

"How did that go?"

"I think he was right to send me there. I was never a drug user before I met Danny, except for a little pot now and then, so I really didn't know what I was doing. I just thought it was cool fun. The person at the clinic told me their story, which started out just like mine and ended with a criminal record and homelessness. I'm going to see the counselor again and take some classes, but I already made up my mind I'm not playing with this stuff again, especially after what I did to you."

"Stop that. It wasn't you. It was me and I got what I deserved. Did you tell Danny?"

"Yeah, I told him what Darell said and asked if he would come see the counselor with me. I thought he was going to punch me, he was so pissed. I'm giving him up for good too. Maybe I'll grow up some day and make better choices."

"Me too," said Vicki. "Me too."

That afternoon Vicki told Dr. Justice about her dream.

"Could your mind be telling you that door is closed?"

"I don't know, maybe."

She also told him the Amy story. "She thought she was sharing a little fun thing she'd discovered. She had no idea what I was going to do with it."

"She had to know it was wrong to give it to you."

"She did, but she thought it was harmless."

"What do you think about her decision to stop using it and ditch the boyfriend who got her started?"

"Honestly, my first selfish thought was that would keep me out of any legal trouble. My second thought was how simply she was able to say, 'That's it, I won't do those things anymore.' How come I wasn't that smart?"

"We learn in different ways."

"Do you think my dream is trying to teach me the Portal is closed to me?"

"Write that down in your journal. We'll pick up there tomorrow morning."

DAY THREE

RICHARD AND AUDREY AND ELIZABETH showed up for the morning visitor shift on Thursday.

"I brought the whole family," said Audrey.

"Not quite, where's Lincoln?"

"You'll have to make do with the stuffed one for now. Without a therapy dog vest, he's not welcome here."

"Well at least let me hold Elizabeth while we visit."

"Trey says I should try the cinnamon buns," said Richard.

"Go," said Vicki. "And don't hurry back. We girls have some gossip to catch up on."

"We do?" said Audrey as Richard headed off on his quest. Vicki couldn't know Don was going to call, could she?

The gossip was the whole Amy story. Audrey hadn't asked Vicki where she got the drugs, but she knew now. "I wasn't going to tell on her, but Darell figured it out somehow."

"Be thankful it was Darell. You and Amy both could have been in big trouble. I'll bet Lincoln told him."

"Lincoln?"

"Of course. He was the only one that could have known, and he wouldn't have wanted anything bad to happen to you or Amy."

"What do you think, Elizabeth?" she asked the sleeping infant. "I thought he figured it out from the syringe."

"I'm sure he did," Audrey laughed. "I'm kidding, Vicki. Lincoln would never narc on you. What happened to your sense of humor?"

"It waxes and wanes when you're locked up in a mental ward. You should try it some time."

"I'll take your word for it. I do have some gossip for you that will make you feel better."

"Pray tell."

"I took your advice and called Abbey. We're all good. We're friends again."

"That does make me feel better. I love you both. We're all connected in a special way that most people could never understand. I'm glad we can be the Three Musketeers again."

Richard returned with fresh coffee and more cinnamon buns. "Trey was right, I'm stealing some of these."

"I warned Trey. You guys are going to get fat. At least remember to wait an hour before getting in the pool."

"Speaking of the pool, Trey thinks I'm getting good enough that we should look at scuba certification and a diving vacation for the gang."

"Trey was afraid of the water just a few months ago and now he's Jacque Cousteau?" said Vicki.

"Just a thought."

Vicki's phone started vibrating on the nightstand.

"It's Don," she said, handing Elizabeth to Audrey.

"Don!" answered Vicki. "How did you find me?"

"You can run but you can't hide. I have informants everywhere. I have you on speaker phone, so watch your language. Abbey is with me."

"We wouldn't want to offend Abbey," she laughed. "I'm putting you guys on speaker phone, so watch your language. Richard and Audrey and Elizabeth are here with me."

"Good, then we won't have to tell this story over and over. I'll never question your intuition again. We found Isabel. She was right where you said she'd be, scattered in clay all over the Stonehenge field. The DNA match came in overnight."

"One of us isn't surprised," said Vicki.

"Make that two," said Audrey.

"Three," added Abbey.

"Does that close your case?" asked Richard.

"Essentially, yes," responded Don. "We no longer have a missing person and the purported assailant, already linked by DNA, is deceased. I'm not sure anyone would believe where the hunch came from to reinvestigate the scene, but we'll leave the official record at that, a hunch."

"I have a gift for you Vicki," said Abbey. "We had a lot more evidence than the lab needed, so I kept a cup of the clay stuff. The evidence guy said the DNA should be in all the granules, so you can meet the real Isabel in person the next time we get together."

Vicki hadn't heard the bell in some time, but it went off now.

MORNING SESSION WITH DR. TOM

"THAT'S REMARKABLE," SAID TOM WHEN HE heard Vicki's news about Isabel. "Our book together will have a compelling new chapter from that."

"Does that mean you believe everything, and I can go home now?"

"I've believed in you since we first met. I can't give documented scientific evidence to support that, but I do believe. Sending you home requires me to know that you won't continue to be a danger to yourself. We're still working on that. Let's revisit the Amy story and yesterday's dream and go from there. What if your dream was your subconscious telling you the Portal was closed to you? Have you given any more thought to that?"

"What do you think?"

"That I'm supposed to be the one asking the questions and you're deflecting. Since you ask, though, I'll tell you how I see the two things as related. Amy was engaging in something she thought was harmlessly chasing a unique and possibly enlightening experience. When confronting the conceivable consequences of incarceration or homelessness, even though she had not experienced any penalty herself, she made a choice to no longer expose herself to that potential harm. You seemed impressed with her ability to say she was simply going to quit things that she had learned were harmful to her. Do you think that is a good choice?"

"Yes."

"I think the Portal is a similar draw for you, but in your case, you have experienced actual penalties to a life-threatening degree, yet still you seem to want to revisit the experience. Do you think that is a good choice?"

Silence, no eye contact.

"Vicki, do you believe in God?"

"I believe in spirituality, I'm not really religious."

"Do you believe in a supreme spirit? One entity as the source, meaning, and sustaining presence of all that exists?"

"Maybe. I don't really think about it."

"Then I'll ask you to cancel your visitors for the day and think about it. Your assignment is to take your journal and find a quiet spot for that. I'll ask you again when we get together at 2:00."

Vicki left, puzzled.

She called Trey and Darell to let them know they didn't need to stop by because she had homework to do. She also let them know about Don's findings.

The library was empty and quiet. Vicki stared at a blank page in her journal and called Audrey.

"Audrey, do we believe in God?"

"That's a weird question we never explored before. I do. I guess I assumed you did too. Don't you? You believe in something that sends you signals and gives you gifts. Isn't that God?"

"I don't know. I believe in a spirit world, but Dr. Justice asked if I believed in one supreme spirit. The foster parents in my group home talked about God that way all the time."

"I think God put Richard and Elizabeth in my life. And you too."

"What about Clyde? He was in your life before Richard. Did God kill him?"

"I thought about that a lot at the time. I was angry with God for letting him die that way. I thought my life was over and I'd never be happy again. I asked God why it happened."

"Did God answer?"

"Not in words, but I think so now. As time passed, I stopped fighting and started painting again. I spent more time with you and the store and started teaching my classes, which led me to meet Richard. Now I thank God that I was able to let it go and have faith that it was how things were meant to be. When I met Richard, I knew it was the right thing. How did you know Trey was the right thing for you?"

"I just did. I knew it right away."

"I think that's how it works. How did you and I come to be? How did you get your spiritual gifts? How did you grow up with no family and become a smart independent entrepreneur? How did you not die on the boat that day? Don't you think there must be something watching and guiding your life?"

"You believe that's God."

"I do. When I think back on every choice, every bad experience I have had that taught me a lesson, every boyfriend I thought I was in love with, every class I took, meeting you, I know that things wouldn't be what they are today if they went the way I thought they should go. There must be something greater than me that guides that in the right way. I believe that's God. When I have faith and trust in that, I find that better things come into my life than anything I could have imagined. That doesn't mean that bad things never happen, but when I look back, I can see that all of it happens for a reason."

"Maybe I need to talk to God?"

"I always thought you did talk to God. Every time you had that special intuition, when you put your faith in visions or crystals or what comes through a séance, I thought that was you and God. I guess that's why we've never had this conversation before. I always thought you were more connected to God than anyone I've known."

"And I always thought we just had a special extra sense, a gift from the universe. I never thought to label it as God. My last foster parents made me believe that God was embodied in religion and ritual. The spiritual experiences I've had were not bound by any of that. They had to be something different than God."

"Maybe you could try asking God?"

Vicki made a lot of notes after her talk with Audrey. She returned to her room, got down on her knees by the bed and said out loud, "I've never done this before but I'm trying it now. God if you are there, if you do exist, help me to believe and trust in you." And slept.

2:15

THE KNOCK ON THE DOOR WAS DR. JUSTICE.
"I was worried about you," he said as Vicki opened her eyes. "It's not like you to be late."

She looked at the clock. Two hours had passed since she talked to Audrey.

"Sweet dreams I hope?"

Odd. She hadn't dreamed at all and didn't even remember sleeping. She was wide awake. Where had she been? "Sorry," she said with an embarrassed smile.

"It's okay, good rest is a good thing," Tom said, looking at all the journal notes added since this morning. "You've been working hard. You look pretty comfy with your pillows and your stuffed dog. Shall we do our session right here?"

She hadn't even noticed that she was hugging faux Lincoln. *"God is dog spelled backwards."* That was a silly thought, and she laughed.

"Did I say something funny?"

"No, I thought something funny. God is dog spelled backwards." She laughed again.

"I was going to start by asking if you believed in God," he laughed with her. "Is that your final answer?"

"Is it a good one?"

"I can't say it's the deepest reflection I've heard on the subject, but it's a positive one. People often find their pets to be a source of unconditional love. Many see God in the same way."

"I asked Audrey if we believed in God. She does, and she thinks I do too."

"What do you think?"

"I think I've been confused. I thought God was Church. Audrey says God is everything mystical I've ever believed in all along."

"Does that sound right?"

"It makes sense to me. I think it's possible that God is the light of the Portal."

"That would be consistent with the thousands of cases that Dr. Long has documented. I believe you had a similar sense of welcoming love that others report. Could that be dog spelled backwards?"

"I think Audrey's right. I do believe in God. I just didn't know it."

"Now that you know it, does it change anything?"

"It changes everything. It means that every stray supernatural nudge came from one place, and it was a place of love trying to help me. Why couldn't I feel that on my own?"

"You had an uncommon series of early life experiences with no stability in parents, family, friends, or role models. You had to make your own sense of what life was and what guided it. We're not well equipped to do that with our child and adolescent brains. You were all you had to work with. Maybe God was trying to help by sending you intuition that others didn't have, but you weren't able to surrender to it then."

"So, God made a mistake with me?"

"Not at all. He just allowed you to learn in different ways. Your life has still turned out better than most, and the best could be ahead if you're ready to surrender to it now."

"What do I need to do?"

"Nothing."

"Nothing?"

"Do you remember Dr. Cole saying that only God should be playing God? God's name is not Vicki for a reason. All you have to do is let him drive the bus. Trust that the bus driver knows the right way to go. That doesn't mean you won't get off at the wrong stop now and then, but you can always get back on knowing that it will always follow the correct route."

"I guess the other day was a wrong stop."

"I don't think there was a stop that day. For some reason you just chose to jump out into freeway traffic. Would you do that again today?"

"No."

"Do you think you're ready to give up on going back to the Portal?"

"I think so, yes."

"What about your stabbing plan?"

"I knew I shouldn't have told you about that. I don't want to get off the bus in that neighborhood anymore."

"Good to hear. Meet me in my office tomorrow morning at 10:00."

When Tom got back to the office he called Trey's cell phone.

"Dr. Justice, is everything okay?"

"Quite. Can you be here tomorrow at 9:00 a.m. for a quick visit?"

"Sure, whatever you need."

"Vicki is scheduled to be in my office at her regular meeting time tomorrow morning. I wanted to visit with you before then and go over a couple of things before I release her into your care. She'll continue meeting with me, but I'm comfortable that we can do that on an outpatient basis. She doesn't know this yet. She'll find out tomorrow at 10:00."

"Are you sure she's ready to come home?"

"I am. I'll share my assessment with you in the morning. I believe she's had an epiphany. I'll let her tell you about it."

HAPPY DAYS ARE HERE AGAIN

"YESTERDAY YOU ASKED ME IF I WAS SURE your wife was ready to come home. Are you ready to have her home?" said Dr. Justice to Trey.

"I miss her, but I'm afraid of doing this all over again in another month."

"That's a legitimate concern. Can you trust her again?"

"I want to."

"You need to without doubt. You're her primary support for putting this episode behind her."

"Is it behind her?"

"The risk is never zero. We evaluate it as low, moderate, or high in terms of potential harm to oneself or others. When she arrived here, it was unquestionably high and there was no responsible alternative to hospitalization. She never had suicidal thoughts in the classic sense, but the thoughts she did have about her choices put her in danger of the same outcome. I'm glad you helped her make the right choice and she was able to stay here with us. I'm not sure she could have progressed so rapidly with strangers in a forced institutional setting.

"From our first meeting with you and her friends, I was inclined to label the risk as moderate. Staying here was still the right choice, but it was clear she had a strong relationship base. She accepted that you all believed this was in her best interest, and her mental state has been stable. All of you have continued to engage with her in supportive ways through the past several days of treatment. These are important protective factors for the patient. They don't erase risk, but they do buffer it. She has also shown rapid progress in her spiritual and personal beliefs about the choices she has made and expressed new resolve to not repeat those decisions.

"Based on all of these factors, I would assess her current risk level as low and release her from hospital custody. That doesn't mean we're done. I would also insist on agreement to ongoing therapy on an outpatient basis with an open time-line based on continued progress. Do you have any questions about the assessment or treatment plan?"

Trey wiped away a tear. "I want Vicki back so badly, the Vicki I knew before all of this Portal thing happened."

"We're all taking a leap of faith here."

As the next month passed, it proved to be the right leap. The unruffled, lighthearted, irreverent Vicki was back in the Peacock Plume. Trey was overwhelmed by an overload of buttered buns. When not gloriously dying from cinnamon poisoning brought on by Vicki's seemingly insatiable pent-up demands, he and Richard were finalizing new plans for further scope creep in the Peacock Plume renovation project. Audrey and Elizabeth were also by Vicki's side as Audrey scheduled some wine drinking/painting classes at the gallery in the Peacock Plume.

The band was back together again and the music was sweet, until ...

Michele arrived at the shop early as usual one morning. When Trey and Vicki came down to join morning coffee, Michele announced, "I have some bad news. Michael's not here because he's packing to catch a flight. His sister called and said if he wanted to see his mother alive one more time, he had to come right away."

"Oh no," said Vicki. "I knew she hadn't been well. I had no idea it was that close.'

"None of us did."

"What can we do to help?" asked Trey.

"I'm afraid you'll have to run the store without us. I feel crummy abandoning you without notice, but I want to start the drive up to join him."

"You need to do that," said Vicki. "Don't worry about the shop."

"It won't be a problem at all. We'll close it," said Trey. The two women looked at him in surprise.

"Close it?" said Michele.

"Not forever, but sure, why not? All the regular customers know we've been planning to do it for some time. We'll put out a week's notice and turn it over to the contractors for a month. No time like the present. Maybe you'll be back for the grand reopening."

"I wish I could promise that. Michael is the executor on the will, and the house passes to him. It's an old oceanfront cottage. We love it here, but we had once planned to live there when the time came. I don't know what he'll want to do when everything is settled."

"It doesn't matter," said Vicki. "Whatever is supposed to happen will happen. I believe that."

"I do too," said Trey. "Don't have any worries about anything here. You need to be with your husband now."

"Thanks, friends. We love you both."

When Michele was gone, Trey hugged Vicki and said, "This is one of those God things you've been telling me about."

"It is."

The next week passed quickly as the Peacock Plume prepared to become a phoenix rising from the ashes. Vicki's outpatient sessions with Dr. Justice had become book planning sessions by now, and he blessed Trey's plans for some time off.

"We're out of here," said Trey. "Richard's got all of the construction stuff under control, and I'm ready for a road trip with my best friend and lover."

"Which one am I?" asked Vicki.

"The smartass one."

"I still have no idea where we're going."

"That's part of the fun. You get to guess along the way. I've got the first week nailed, but we're gypsies after that. Who cares as long as it's just us."

Trey turned right out of the shop heading east on 236. "I guess we're not spending the first week in Fairfax?"

"You're really good at this game," Trey laughed.

In between chit chat, Vicki called out geographic clues. "395 South, not going to DC."

As they crossed the 495 Capital Beltway, 395 became I95 South. "I'm ruling out Baltimore, Eastern Shore, and Shenandoah Valley, next possible highlight is Fredericksburg."

Fredericksburg was a stop for eliminating morning coffee and loading up giant Dr. Peppers, but the trip continued. "Twizzlers and beef jerky please," Trey requested. "We still have a way to go. Any more guesses?"

"Probably not Kings Dominion or Richmond, maybe Williamsburg? I love Williamsburg."

"Me too. I've always thought we'd like to stay in one of the colonial homes or tavern rooms in the historic district. Let's see if you're right." I95S to 64E. Williamsburg seemed promising until they passed it.

"Very clever ruse. You're just messing with me now," said Vicki. "Virginia Beach is possible, but you could always take the Bay Bridge Tunnel, which opens the Eastern Shore and Chincoteague." Vicki was reading off trivia questions from her phone to kill time when Trey turned off at I68S. "Game over," she said excitedly. "We're going to Nag's Head!"

"Ding, ding, ding, we have a winner! I got the inspiration from Michele talking about an oceanfront cottage."

"Dinner tonight at Owen's?"

"You know it."

By tradition they avoided "asshole alley," taking the beach road all the way to South Nags Head. Trey clicked into four-wheel drive for the last 100 yards as they churned out onto the beach to arrive at a house on stilts standing alone, all its neighbors washed away by previous storms. Buttered buns turned out predictably to be a bad idea for sex in the sand, but they were in love and at peace.

A QUIET NIGHT

PEACE HAD ALSO SETTLED ON THE HIS-
toric Craft home. Family and friends went through a lot in the
past years and months, but the most recent weeks had been
pleasantly uneventful, and it seemed all was settling nicely.

Michael and Michele were back in New England for the
foreseeable future. Richard was overseeing Peacock Plume
construction. Darell was solving crimes and finishing his
studies for retirement transition in another year. In his spare
time, he was also standing in for Trey continuing Richard's
swimming classes.

The most conflicted person had been Vicki, but she had
been healthy and energized after her most recent hospital
incident that scared everyone. Vicki had sworn off the Portal
journey, and she and Trey were off on a serene break.

Elizabeth slept soundly in her new nursery with Lincoln
by her side. Richard and Audrey had donned their big fleecy
robes and settled onto the big couch in the great room with
glasses of wine. A warm fire burned in the fireplace, and the
baby monitor was quiet beside them on the end table. The
shadows of a moonless night were beautiful and wondrous in
the spotlights on the deck.

"I have not been this comfortable and happy for some time," spoke Richard.

Audrey sipped her wine and stared at the fire. "It is pretty special."

"What do you think about the vacation plans Trey and Darell and I are working on?"

"I'm not thinking about them at all tonight. This is the first time we've been alone in months. I have something else on my mind," she said with a seductive smile. "We've been sadly neglecting our marital duties, and I'd like to make up for lost time."

"What do you mean neglecting our marital duties? I take out the trash twice a week and all the bills are paid."

"Good, big boy, but tonight I want something more from you." She put down the wine glass, took his head in both hands and pulled him to her for a long, deep wet kiss.

"So demanding."

"Oh, we're just getting started." Audrey rose and went to the big furry rug in front of the fireplace. Turning to Richard, she opened her robe and dropped it onto the floor. She had shed the postpartum weight, and her body was magnificent as ever, enhanced now with milk-swollen breasts and beckoning erect nipples.

"You're not wearing pajamas."

"Is that a problem?"

"Maybe not," he said rising and dropping his robe. "I'll try to catch up." He quickly ditched the robe and sock monkey flannels and headed her way, very obviously prepared for deeper exploration.

The wetness and deepness of the kisses escalated. The lovers' hands explored every mound and crevice as they sank to the floor and entwined on the soft rug warm from the fire. They silently morphed into a position that granted mutual oral access for unhurried pleasures of tongues and lips. Audrey stopped with a gasp and a light convulsion as she soaked the carpet in ecstasy. "I think I'm ready for you," she said in an embarrassed laugh.

"I know I'm ready for you." He rose up to mount and entered her damp warmth, slowly teasing at first before surrendering to a deep coupling. The fire crackled and their bodies were slick with sweat as they moved together, lips touching with soft licks and whispers of love. The dance quickened as Audrey hugged him tighter and pulled him in further, arching her pelvis aggressively. She was breathing heavily with soft moaning that grew to a scream as her body shuddered in acceptance of Richard's grunting explosion. He continued kissing her as they slowed to a rest and her quivering lessened to a satisfied calm.

They lay like that for several minutes and might have stayed that way for hours if not for Lincoln, making his rounds, sticking his cold nose in Richard's butt.

"Yikes!" Richard exclaimed, rapidly uncoupling. He flipped onto his back as Lincoln pranced around the scene of the crime and Audrey laughed loudly. "That was rude," he said to the dog as Lincoln snorted and briefly laid down close against Audrey before making a final round and heading back upstairs to Elizabeth.

"He's probably jealous," said Richard.

"Wait until he hears Round Two," said Audrey softly and seductively.

"I don't know, I may be a one-trick pony after that."

"Let's see," said Audrey as she gathered the few articles of clothing, signaling that Richard should follow her upstairs.

Still warm from the fire, Audrey pulled down the blanket. Without a sound she slipped under the single sheet, her hands and mouth actively coaxing the desired reaction. She mounted him this time, her breasts soft on his chest and her hair falling around his face, kissing him as she rode them to another climax and a deep sleep.

A NEW DAY

RICHARD WOKE EARLY, AS ALWAYS, PULLED on his robe and slippers, and headed to the kitchen to start the coffee. The evening's pleasures were fresh in his mind, thanking his maker for the amazing gift of Audrey. It was odd that Lincoln hadn't joined him yet, but he must have decided to sleep in. Or he was still jealous and pouting, thought Richard with a smile.

He left the door open as he took the first cup of coffee to the front porch, its steam rising like a waving prayer flag in the crisp morning air. Another beautiful day to love my wife and family. This is truly the best of times.

Then he heard the barking. The sound was coming from down the driveway. Setting his cup on the porch rail, he went to see what was happening beyond the tree line, gravel crunching under his slippers.

As the view opened to the end of the road, the barking became more insistent, and he saw the source of the sound. It was Lincoln, frantic and jumping, his leash tying him to the fence ahead.

"How did you get here?" he said, looking around and seeing no one, as he approached and untied a long unfamiliar leash.

"Let's get you back where you belong." Lincoln tugged wildly as they headed back to the house. "Stop it, you're going to trip me." His mind was racing through possible explanations when the worst thought struck him and he broke into a run. "Go, Lincoln." Richard dropped the leash, and the sheltie raced far ahead and through the open door, sounding his alarm all the way. "Audrey," Richard yelled as he ran out of his slippers and up the gravel drive. "Audrey! Elizabeth," he shouted repeatedly, awkwardly tripping on the front steps and recovering to sprint down the hall and up the stairs.

Audrey had gotten up shortly after Richard. She was dressed and lazily enjoying last night's memories when all the noise started. Richard ran past their bedroom doorway, still shouting, and she quickly followed him to Elizabeth's room where Lincoln was now whimpering.

The crib was empty.

AFTERMATH

DARELL WAS IN HIS HOME OFFICE STUDYING
for a test when the phone buzzed. Without looking, he picked
it up and answered, "Sergeant Metz."

"Darell," said Richard. "It happened. Elizabeth is gone."

"Gone," he said, processing what he was hearing. "Have
you called 911?"

"Of course!"

"Good, patrol will secure the scene, and a detective will be
assigned. I'll make some calls and find out who that will be,
and I'll get there as soon as I can. How is Audrey?"

"Quiet, we're both just stunned. And don't know where
to start."

"Don't do anything until I get there. Do you need me to
make any calls for you?"

"You're the only call I've made after 911."

"Then just try to stay calm. I'll let Vicki and Trey know
what's going on."

"Thanks."

The patrol car arrived. Richard met the officer in the
driveway. "Sergeant Metz is a close friend of the family,"
Richard said. "He's on his way."

"The 911 report was for a missing child. Is the child still missing?"

"Yes, she is."

"Let's start with a description so I can get an alert out. She may have just wandered off and be close by."

"She's just an infant. She can't even walk yet. Someone had to have taken her."

"Sorry, now I understand. When did you last see her?"

"Last night when we went to bed."

"We? There is someone else with you?"

"Yes, my wife. She's in the house."

"Anyone else? Other family?"

"No, just us."

"This is your daughter that's missing?"

"Yes."

"Can you tell me approximately what time you or your wife last saw her?"

Richard realized they hadn't seen Elizabeth since tucking her in and heading downstairs. They didn't check on her when they went to bed. "Around 9:00 p.m."

"And when did you realize she was gone?"

"About 6:00 this morning."

"A nine-hour window," said the officer thinking out loud. "As soon as I call this in, I'll need you to show me where the child was last seen."

"I'll get my wife and we can meet inside."

"Did I hear a dog barking?"

"Yes, that's Lincoln, and he's friendly. You can walk right in."

"Was the dog here all night?"

"Yes."

"Good to know. I'll find you inside in just a minute."

They were talking in the kitchen when Darell arrived. He knew the officer. "Good to see you, Jim," Darell said.

"You too, sorry about the circumstances. I understand you're a family friend."

"Unfortunately shit happens. Audrey, Richard, I talked to Trey. He and Vicki will be back this evening. Jim, what have you gotten so far?"

"Missing infant, discovery 6:00 a.m., last seen 9:00 p.m., parents, two adults, and family pet, dog, present through that window of time. That's about it."

"Would you like me to stay with Audrey while Richard shows you the crime scene so you can start securing it?"

"That would be helpful until someone else arrives."

"This way," said Richard, taking the officer upstairs.

"Darell, I'm so glad you're here," said Audrey, crying and hugging him tightly.

"I wouldn't want to be anywhere else right now. Let's find a more comfortable spot. This may take some time."

After settling in the great room, "Audrey, let me explain to you what's going on. Jim's first task is to secure the initial scene quickly, so it doesn't get all trampled over as other officers arrive. Everything will be photographed in detail there, and he'll be asking Richard about other potential areas of interest, entry and exit points, anything out of place, etc. As other officers arrive, those areas will also be secured and photographed, and nothing will be touched until the forensics folks begin taking measurements and gathering evidence.

"Next, we need all witness statements. You're with me right now because we need to keep the witnesses separated. I don't want to scare or upset you, but you need to know that you and Richard are not only witnesses but suspects at this point."

"Suspects?" Audrey jumped up and threw her hands in the air. "Oh my God, my daughter is gone." She stared angrily out the window, then turned back to Darell. "Shouldn't someone be trying to find her already?"

"Family is always suspect. It's not personal, and don't worry, I'm sure they'll clear you and Richard as soon as they get your witness statements."

"Should I tell them about the warning that Elizabeth was going to be kidnapped?" Audrey said through sobs. "I didn't believe it was real. I can't believe I didn't check on her. I should have kept her with us every minute!"

"Tell them everything you know."

Over the next two hours, additional patrol officers and forensic techs appeared and recorded details of all potential sites of interest. Darell was still with Audrey when the investigating detective arrived and introduced herself. "Mrs. Craft, I'm Detective Anne Bishop with the Special Victims Unit." To Darell, "Sergeant Metz, I understand you're a family friend."

"I am, and I'm glad to see you got the call for this one. Now that the wagons are circled, I'm going to get myself out of the way. Audrey, you're in good hands here. I'll check in with you and Richard later today."

"Thanks, Darell."

"Mrs. Craft, I know this is a difficult time for you, but it's also a critical time for our investigation. I need to get your witness statement on the events of the last 24 hours."

"I understand." The tears continued. "Darell said family members are the first suspects but shouldn't someone be looking for Elizabeth?" She looked down at her empty hands feeling helpless.

"Did you and your husband have anything to do with your daughter's disappearance?"

"No!" Audrey's head whipped up. "How can you even suggest that?"

"I understand this is very upsetting. We want to eliminate you as suspects quickly and get to finding your daughter. When did you last see her?"

Audrey's story matched Richard's. The times were the same, and they both acknowledged a few glasses of wine. They were together the whole time and noticed no noises from the baby monitor. Further probing from Detective Bishop also surfaced some strenuous activity before bedtime that might have contributed to a sounder than normal sleep for both.

"Thank you for your candid responses, I reviewed your husband's statement earlier and have no concerns clearing you both from the suspect list. We've already released an Amber

Alert. A grid search of your property is being organized, and officers are going door to door in the surrounding area. Is there anything else you can tell me that might be helpful to our search?"

"Maybe. We were told a couple of months ago that our daughter was going to be kidnapped."

"Did you report that to us at that time?"

"No, we didn't think anyone would take it seriously."

"Why not?"

Through sobs, "The source was a dead woman, a spirit from a séance."

BACK TO VIRGINIA

THEY WERE A FEW HOURS INTO THE DRIVE north when Trey asked Vicki, "What are you thinking?"

"That Isabel knows the answer. I know I swore off going back to the Portal, but I have to."

"That's what I was afraid of. Thanks for being honest, but you know I can't let you do that, even if it means putting you back in the psych ward."

"What else can I do?"

"Have you tried praying? You talked a lot about God when you first got out of there. Did you mean it?"

"I did but I'm not sure now. Why would he take Elizabeth?"

"God didn't take Elizabeth."

"Fine," Vicki said getting agitated. "God let Elizabeth be taken. Why?"

Trey wasn't sure if he was going to be angry with her, but he felt a calm come over him as he said, "I don't know but maybe we're not supposed to know. Maybe we're just supposed to trust that God has a reason for everything."

"Isabel knows."

The rest of the drive was quiet. It was close to 6:00 p.m. when they got to their destination. Trey drove past crime scene tape on the front fence and along the driveway and pulled up to park by the porch. Richard opened the front door as they were getting out of the truck, and Lincoln was the first to greet them.

"Hi, baby," said Vicki, hugging the dog. "I know you're missing your sister."

Audrey came out for Vicki's second hug. Richard would normally greet Trey with a manly fist bump. This time he grabbed him in a bone crushing hug of gratitude, wiping tears on Trey's chest. They said nothing. They all walked inside, passing more crime tape in the hall and on the stairway.

Trey spoke first when they were standing in the kitchen. It wasn't much. "I don't know what to say."

"Thanks for being here," said Richard.

"What can we do?" Trey said to Audrey.

"I don't know," she responded, her eyes red and puffy from the tears. "We're waiting for Darell to tell us if there's any news."

"I think waiting is the same as wasting time," said Richard, "I feel so helpless." He said running his hands through his hair repeatedly. "God damn it! I need a drink. Anyone else?"

Audrey and Vicki answered affirmatively. Trey said, "I'll have a beer." And they went to the great room to sit by the fire and wait.

Darell walked in just before 7:00. He had a handful of crime scene tape. "I pulled this from the driveway," he said. "Forensics is done here so we can take down all the confetti."

"Any news?" asked Audrey expectantly.

"I had a call with Detective Bishop. She's on the lookout for another witness, a dead woman from a séance." Darell laughed. No one else laughed.

"I know how to get in touch with her," said Vicki.

"We're not going there," said Trey firmly. "Have the police found anything else to go on?" he asked Darell.

"Nothing. The weather has been dry for days so there were no footprints or tire tracks left behind. No tool marks or signs of forced entry. Also, no fingerprints, hair, or fibers that aren't consistent with occupants."

"Isn't that unusual?"

"It is but not unheard of. TV shows and social media do a pretty good job of educating smart criminals. Fortunately, most criminals aren't smart, so we usually have a lot of evidence. So far in this case, nothing."

"Ghosts never leave evidence," offered Vicki.

"Given the history of this house," said Darell. "I rule out nothing, but I don't expect that will turn up as a working theory in Detective Bishop's reports."

Audrey had been pacing the room. She stopped. "What happens now? We have to find Elizabeth!" she shouted.

"I'm with you Audrey but unless Lincoln wants to share his knowledge, the leads are limited. There is no breaking and entering or physical evidence, but that says something. It would suggest someone familiar with the property rather than a random actor. That theory is further strengthened by the presence of Lincoln. He would be expected to be protective of Elizabeth and he's rarely quiet, especially for a stranger. The profile focus would now move to friends and family, all of us, for a start."

"So, we should expect to be interviewed?" asked Trey.

"Probably not. They've already eliminated Richard and Audrey, and the rest of us have solid alibis. Unless something new turns up, it's a dead end at the moment."

"Amy?" said Vicki. "I don't seriously think she would be involved, but who else fits the profile?"

Darell pondered that a second. "She knows the house and she knows Lincoln, what would be her motive?"

"None really, but when I took Lincoln for grooming, she said her biological clock was ticking."

"Maybe nothing. I'll check her for an alibi."

The next day something new showed up.

SOMETHING OLD, SOMETHING NEW

TREY AND VICKI WERE STAYING WITH Richard and Audrey. Their apartment was a construction zone along with everything else at the Peacock Plume.

The morning started early. Richard and Audrey held each other through the night, but sleep was elusive for all. No one felt like breakfast today. Finally, Trey took charge of the despondent group. "We all need to move," he said. "We can't do anything about Elizabeth until we hear more from Darell, but we can try to take care of ourselves while we wait and the best way to do that is to stay occupied. If the police need to tell us anything we all have cell phones. Richard, you're coming with me. We're going to check on construction and put in some time at the YMCA pool. Audrey, Vicki will stay with you, but you need to draw or paint or do anything that keeps your hands and mind busy."

"There must be something we can do here. What if you and I start going door to door to see if neighbors saw or heard anything?" said Richard.

"You know the police are already doing that. You've even got a cop permanently assigned just to sit in your driveway. We'd only be in the way. We need to get ourselves out of the way and trust them to do their job. They'll call if anything changes. Sitting around feeling helpless and depressed is no good for Elizabeth or any of us. We need to stay occupied."

Audrey spoke, "I have a good friend that says, 'Move a muscle, change a thought.' Maybe you're right."

They all knew he was right. "Okay," said Trey, "get cleaned up and dressed for the day and let's get busy."

When Trey and Richard had left, Audrey was puttering in her attic art studio. Vicki joined her with coffee.

"I called the shrink and told him what happened. He wants to see me this morning," said Vicki. "Would you come with me to help convince him I need to go back to Isabel?"

"Yes! I'll come. Let's go right now! I'd do anything to get Elizabeth back."

"I don't see any other way that we're going to find her."

"I called Abbey this morning. She and Don heard from Darell yesterday that Elizabeth was gone. I told her I was afraid you were going to harm yourself again."

"I'm not. I won't do anything to myself. I just want him to put me back to sleep safely."

"You know he won't do that. Vicki, do you remember when you actually met Isabel for the first time?"

"After the boat accident. She was the shadow that followed me in the Portal."

"But when did she actually contact you? Wasn't it the séance?"

Vicki looked confused.

"It was," said Audrey. "Abbey reminded me of that today."

Confused turned to thoughtful.

"Why don't we do another séance at Stonehenge with Abbey? You don't have to risk harming yourself again."

"It wasn't the same as being with her in the Portal. I can be there with her."

"But it worked. Please Vicki we've got to try it!" Audrey's voice was raised, "Someone could be hurting Elizabeth right now!"

"But I wouldn't be with Isabel."

"Is it more important to you to be in the Portal than to try this? To just get the information we need to get Elizabeth back. I'm already missing my daughter. I don't want to lose you too. Isabel will be with us. Abbey has her remains."

"I don't know if it would work."

"You don't know that it won't if you don't even help Abbey and I try. You need to give up on the Portal or it's going to kill you. I know it. I don't know how I know it, but I feel it for certain."

They stared at each other for a long time before Vicki broke the silence.

"Will you still go to see Dr. Justice with me?"

"Let's go. I'll text Richard to let him know where we are."

They were still at the hospital when Trey and Richard returned home.

"Stop in the driveway," said Richard. "I want to check the mail."

"I think you're getting to be as good a swimmer as I am," said Trey as they got to the kitchen and Richard sorted the envelopes.

Richard smiled at the comment. "Believe me, swimming right now is the last thing on my mind. That's also a pretty low bar considering neither one of us could even float a few months ago."

"I still think Lloyd Bridges would be impressed with our progress."

"Wow, I didn't think you were old enough for that reference." Richard stopped sorting the mail and held out a single piece. "What do you make of this?" It was a sealed USPS envelope with no markings or address.

"I get a lot of junk mail, but it usually says, 'or occupant' at least."

Richard opened it and unfolded the single page inside. "Oh no," he said as he dropped it on the table.

It was four words constructed in the basic serial killer font of mismatched letters cut from periodicals: "the baby is safe."

DR. JUSTICE

TOM WAS ON THE PHONE WHEN VICKI AND Audrey appeared at the office door. "Call you back later?" he said to the receiver and hung up.

"That was Dr. Cole. I let him know what has happened. Vicki, I didn't expect to see you for another month. And Audrey," he said, holding her hands. "I'm glad to see you but sorry about the circumstances. Are you okay?"

"Not really, but when things are bad, Vicki supports me and I support her. It's what we've always done."

"That's an important bond to hold on to."

"There's another bond more important than that right now," said Vicki. "Everything I've told you from the Portal is true, and you know I need to go back now for Elizabeth."

"I don't know that, and you know I will never be a party to that."

Audrey looked pained.

"Audrey, Elizabeth is your daughter. What are your feelings?"

"How the hell do you think I feel?" Audrey shouted. Everyone paused. Quieter now Audrey continued, "I'm sorry Dr. Justice. I'm worried! Anything could be happening to her.

Oh, God! I can't eat or think straight. My stomach is in knots. But it's odd, I also have this feeling that she's still here at the same time."

"Don't be sorry. You have faith that she's still here with you?"

"Yes, I believe she is safe somewhere. She has to be! But the same sense tells me that Vicki is not safe if she tries to go back again. You can't help her do that."

"I won't."

"I believe there's another way."

"What is that?"

"Isabel came to me and Vicki and Abbey and Elizabeth in a Ouija séance. Why wouldn't she come back in the same way? And now we have her physical remains to be present."

"Vicki," he said. "A month or so ago you told me you believed in God. Has that changed?"

"I don't know. Why would he let Elizabeth be kidnapped?"

"You had faith in the Portal when you believed that was going to happen."

"I had faith that I could prevent it."

"Your faith in your power is stronger than your faith in God's power?"

The bell struck so loudly that Vicki's eyes opened wide and she jerked convulsively.

"Are you okay?" asked Tom, suddenly concerned.

"You couldn't hear that?"

"Hear what?"

"The bell, I've never heard it so loud."

"Audrey?" Tom asked. "Did you hear anything?"

"No, but I know Vicki gets these bell messages from time to time. She told me when they started."

"When did they start?"

"When she came home from the boat accident."

"Vicki, you've never told me about a bell. When a patient hears things that others don't, we call that auditory hallucinations. That can be a significant symptom. Can you give me examples of when this has happened?"

"A couple of times I had a message from the Portal or a vision of something I needed to share with someone else. Other times it tells me something important was happening, like when I found out Amy could get me the drug I needed or something about Isabel."

"Why do you think it happened so strongly just now when I asked you if you thought your powers were stronger than God's?"

"I think it just wants me to be ready for something I may have to do."

"Is it a warning?" said Audrey.

WHAT NOW, YOSSARIAN?

DARELL WAS AT THE HOUSE WITH TREY AND Richard when Audrey and Vicki returned. A forensic tech had already taken the note. They would search for fingerprints, sources of the envelope, stationery, letters of the message, and the glue that was used, in hope of turning up additional clues beyond the artifact itself.

Richard showed Audrey and Vicki a picture of the letter. "I started to call you when I got this, but I thought it would be better to wait until we were together."

Audrey stared at the four words. "I felt she was safe, but I won't believe my feelings until I'm holding her in my arms again," said Audrey. "Why can't she be here?"

"Audrey," said Darell. "I like your optimism, but this could be just a delay. We may get an actual ransom note after this."

"Whatever they ask we'll find a way to do it." said Richard.

"Vicki, I followed up on Amy. She has an alibi that I verified with her mother. After she dumped her druggie boyfriend, he started blowing up her phone with texts and voice mails and hanging around the animal shelter and vet clinic. She got

216

scared and moved to her parent's house. She was there when Elizabeth was taken.

"She told me he was mad at her when she asked him about going to the clinic. She thought he was going to hit her. I hope she'll be okay."

"I followed up with the boyfriend. He has a charming accent for someone with such a bad attitude and filthy mouth. He won't be bothering her anymore after I helped him understand the penalties for stalking."

"What do we do now?" asked Trey.

"There's nothing we can do until we get more to go on," responded Darell.

"Vicki and I have something we can do," said Audrey. "We're going back to where we first met Isabel."

Trey took Vicki by the shoulders. "No, you're not. You're not going back to that Portal thing."

"She's not," said Audrey. "Dr. Justice wouldn't let that happen either. We're going back to the Stonehenge field with Abbey. That's where we first met Isabel and where we're going to find her again! Right Vicki?"

"Vicki?" said Trey.

"Audrey and Dr. Justice say I need to have faith. If there's a chance of this trip working, I will."

PENNSYLVANIA

DARELL URGED RICHARD TO STAY BEHIND in case there were any local developments. Trey would be with him.

Darell drove again. It was a quieter trip without Elizabeth. They encountered some hard rain on their drive, but it settled to less than a drizzle by the time they got to Don's house. Don and Abbey were waiting on the porch.

"Audrey," Don said, giving her a hug. "I'm so sorry for what you're going through." She was trembling in his arms, and he felt her tears on his cheek.

"Thanks, Don."

Abbey hugged her next, whispering in her ear, "Welcome back."

"I'm glad to be back with you. Sorry again."

"Nothing to be sorry about, we're moving on."

"How come I don't get any hugs?" said Vicki.

Darell hugged her. "Not what I was looking for," she said, pushing off to get her Don and Abbey hugs.

"Where would you ladies like to start?" asked Don.

"One more introduction," said Abbey, handing Vicki a pint-sized Tupperware container half full of clay granules. "Meet Isabel."

Ding

"Audrey, you're right. This is going to work." Vicki thought to herself, staring into the contents of the plastic bowl. "Good to meet you in the almost flesh," she said out loud.

"Your rooms are ready," said Don. "Let's load what we need for tomorrow in the back of my cruiser and get your other bags inside."

"Can we go now?" asked Audrey.

"Bad idea," said Don, "The drive to the field is rough enough when it's dry and daylight. We've had a lot of rain all day here. A nighttime drive with all the water running off the hill is not going to happen. I hate to disappoint you, but I'll make up for it by hosting tonight at my favorite Italian spot in town. You'll find a plethora of vegetarian alternatives," winking at Vicki.

"I need to pass," said Audrey, "I couldn't eat a thing right now and I want to call Richard."

"I understand," said Don. "If you want to talk later Darell and I will be on the porch with drinks and cigars."

Morning came early.

"Another spectacular Don Weston breakfast feast," said Darell when they were on the way to their destination. "I'm stuffed."

"Do you ladies need anything else for your morning?" asked Don. "I can stop on the way."

"Double-checked everything before breakfast," said Abbey. "We're all good."

"No more delays," said Audrey. "We need to get started."

Don navigated the bumpy, slippery ride into the property and drove past the A-frame and barn remains to the foam rocks of the Stonehenge replica. The stones hadn't changed, but the field still bore the rake marks and the string grid of the Isabel search. The ground had drained remarkably well after yesterday's rain. It was damp but not muddy.

"Will the stakes and twine be in the way?" asked Don. "Darell and I can pull them up for you."

"They won't be a problem," said Abbey. "I'd just leave them there."

"That won't mess with laying out your triangle?" asked Darell.

"We don't need to mark it this time since we already know the right stones to place the crystals on. It's not the string that makes the triangle, it's the crystals."

Don and Darell set up the table and chairs in their previous spot while Vicki distributed the bags of stones. Abbey walked Audrey around the field, scuffing the grass with her foot to show her how they found the pieces of Isabel.

Everyone got quiet and reflective when the Ouija board and the remains of Isabel were set on the table. The salt circle was the last piece. Abbey tried not to think about Elizabeth as she poured that out.

"Time to get the rookies off the field," said Don. "I'm going to let Darell tag along with me for some errands. I should be back in two hours, but text or call if you need us for anything before then."

"Gee, thanks Dad," said Darell.

Hugs and good luck wishes all around and the guys were gone.

The air was still and the field was silent as Vicki, Audrey, and Abbey joined hands across the table.

"We gather here again. This time to ask for help in finding baby Elizabeth," started Vicki. "We reject any negative spirits and welcome all that would help. Isabel, I couldn't come back to you where we last met, so I came to you here. Your body is with us, and we need your spirit to guide us." She surprised herself when she heard her voice closing with, "Please let that be the will of God."

Six hands laid fingers lightly on the planchette and Audrey spoke. "My daughter is missing. Is there anyone here that can help us find her?"

Fifteen seconds that seemed like an hour passed. Jerky twitches began on the board and slowly but surely expanded into sweeping circles of seeming indecision. The planchette settled on YES.

Vicki opened her mouth to speak. Her lips moved but nothing came out. Vicki pulled her hands back from the planchette to settle in her lap, and she laid her head on the table. Audrey and Abbey stared as her head rose again. The face they were looking at wasn't Vicki!

MAY THE TRUTH
BE TOLD

"ISABEL?" GUESSED ABBEY CAUTIOUSLY.

The face and eyes were expressionless, and the voice was halting. "Yes."

"Where is Vicki?"

"She's here."

"Do you know where Elizabeth is?" asked Audrey.

"Yes."

"Why was she kidnapped?"

"She wasn't kidnapped, she was taken for her protection."

"Vicki told us you said Elizabeth was going to be kidnapped."

"I told her a series of unfortunate events were in place that would lead to Elizabeth being taken away."

"I don't understand."

"Neither did she. Everything happens for a reason that we can't know. Some people are blessed with special gifts of intuition from the universe. The wisdom for discernment comes from within. God will grant that if we are still and wait. God knows what we need to learn. We can accept this in faith and the lessons will come to us in serenity, or we can try to take charge of the universe on our own. When we do that, the lessons will still come, but they'll come with a price for our lack of trust. The more independent we try to be from God, the higher the cost."

"Vicki has always been one of the most independent people I know," said Audrey.

"I would have been too. The cost of my chosen pleasures was my life."

"I think Vicki almost made that same choice," said Abbey. "Are we going to lose her?"

"She is part of a much larger plan that she has yet to appreciate. So are you and Audrey and Elizabeth. Trust in the universe, and all will be revealed over your long lives on Earth."

"Are the answers in the Portal?" asked Audrey.

"The answers are in your faith and trust. None of you will see the Portal again until you're called to the light many years away in your time."

"But Vicki was chosen to go the Portal now."

"That was something she didn't understand in her independence and self-will. Those journeys were never about Vicki. That was about me. She was the connection that had to happen for closure of my life on Earth. I can now go in peace to the light."

"What about Elizabeth?"

"Elizabeth is safe. That was one of Vicki's lessons that came at a cost. She chose her will over God's plan. When she couldn't finish what she wanted, the unfortunate incidents were her assumptions and actions. With increasing signs of danger to her and Elizabeth, good Samaritans intervened for Elizabeth's safety, protecting her from the kidnapping threat that never existed."

"Where can I find her?" asked Audrey.

"Vicki knows. She's been with us through all of this. When I leave you now to head to the light, her physical body will be drained, but she'll be back with you. Tell her to focus on the light of peace, and the answer will come to her."

The face went blank as the head slowly dropped to the table. The inert body slumped off the chair and onto the ground, Vicki's face staring blankly at the sky.

WHAT HAPPENED

"DON, COME BACK NOW," ABBEY'S VOICE over the phone was urgent. "Vicki is unconscious."

"Is she breathing?"

"Yes, but we can't wake her."

"We're on the way."

The lights were still flashing on the cruiser when it raced across the fields and slid to a stop at the site of the séance. Darell and Don saw Audrey on her knees. She was hugging Vicki from behind, supporting her in a sitting position. Vicki was conscious now but still not speaking.

"What happened?" asked Don.

Abbey answered, "Isabel was here. She spoke to us through Vicki. When she left, Vicki fell to the ground and I called you."

Audrey was crying as she whispered in Vicki's ear, "I love you. It's over now. Please come back to me. Elizabeth and I need you more than ever."

Vicki blinked her eyes as everyone held their breath. "I'm okay," she said weakly, then louder and stronger, "I'm okay."

"Don't try to get up," said Don. "You're not okay yet. Darell, why don't you pack things up here, and we'll take Vicki back to the house."

By the time the car was loaded, Vicki was up on her feet and talking with Abbey and Audrey. They were telling her everything that happened, and she was saying, "I know, I know. I heard everything." That and "I'm sorry, it was all my fault. I know better now, and I promise I won't scare you like that again."

"Okay," said Don, reaching to help Vicki walk. "Let's get you loaded into the car so we can get you some rest."

Vicki stopped him. "Don, I am 100% fine. I'm wide awake and clear thinking and perfectly capable of walking to the car."

"Suit yourself, just trying to be a gentleman."

Don and Darell sat up front listening to the excited chatter of the three women. As they were nearing Don's house, Abbey asked the big question: "The last time Audrey asked where we could find Elizabeth, Isabel said we were to tell you to focus on the light of peace. She said the answer would come to you. Do you know the answer?"

"Yes, and Trey would too if he were here. I'll explain it when we get inside."

"You know?" said Audrey, "Then tell me, tell me now!"

She did. "And now we need to make a phone call."

HOW ARE THINGS IN NEW ENGLAND?

"MICHELE, IT'S VICKI, HOW IS MICHAEL'S mom doing?"

Hesitation followed by a stammering, "Sh ... she's doing surprisingly well. She's still hanging in there. I thought you and Trey were off on vacation."

"We are, but I've been thinking of you two a lot just recently. How is Elizabeth?"

"Oh, Elizabeth is just fi— ... what do you mean?"

"Aren't you still protecting her?"

 Quiet.

"I'm going to put you on speaker phone now. Audrey and Darell are with me." Vicki continued, "Michael's mother never had an emergency, did she?"

"No," sniffling.

"And you never went to New England, did you?"

"No ... we're at our apartment in Falls Church."

"And Elizabeth?"

"She's well, she's with us."

"Oh my God," shouted Audrey. "You have Elizabeth? You took my daughter?"

"Audrey, I'm so sorry. We took her to save her from the kidnappers. We couldn't tell anyone. We made a note so people would know she was safe, but we couldn't tell anyone where she was so the kidnappers couldn't find her."

"There are no kidnappers." Said Vicki.

"Really?"

"Really, this is all my fault. I made a mistake."

Darell motioned for the phone, and Vicki handed it over.

"Michele, this is Darell Metz. Is Michael with you?"

"Yes, do you want to talk to him?"

"I want to talk to you both."

"Hi Darell," Michael's voice on the speaker.

"I'm sure you two know that Arlington County Police are looking for Elizabeth and whoever took her."

"Yes."

"Can I trust you to take her to her father now?"

"She's safe? There are no kidnappers coming?" Michele's voice.

"She is, but you two may be in some trouble. Take her to Richard now. Trey is with him. We'll be there in a couple of hours to meet you."

"Should we turn ourselves in to the police?" asked Michael. "We thought we were doing the right thing for Elizabeth."

"Please," said Audrey crying, "Please just take my baby home to her father now."

"Just go to the Craft house and stay there." Said Darell. "I need to make some phone calls on the way. Promise me you'll do this, and I'll let you know when I get there if we have to go to the police station. I'll go with you if we need to do that."

"Okay, does Richard know we're coming?"

"He will before you get there. Be safe."

"Thank you," said Michele. "I'm so glad this is over."

"Everyone will be glad when this is over, but it's not over yet. Audrey and Vicki and I will be there soon."

Don and Abbey had stayed quiet through the call. Darell hung up and said, "Gotta go, Don, thanks for the hospitality." Hugs all around as the car was loaded and they were off.

PHONE CALLS

VICKI INSISTED ON DRIVING. AUDREY AND Darell were making phone calls.

The first was on speaker phone to Richard and Trey. "Richard," Audrey said. "Michele and Michael are on their way to see you. They have Elizabeth, and she's safe."

"Thank God she's safe. Where has she been. How did they find her?" asked Richard.

"I thought they were in New England with Michael's mom," said Trey.

"That was a good alibi," said Darell. "But they never left Falls Church. They had her the whole time. They took her to protect her from the kidnappers, but there never were any kidnappers. It gets a little complicated, but everyone is safe, and we'll be there in two hours to join you. Hug your daughter, and we'll sort it all out when we get there."

"It's really all okay now," said Audrey. She was still distraught herself but was trying to be composed and positive as possible for Richard. "We talked to Michael and Michele. They were only trying to help. Elizabeth has been safe the whole time. She's coming home now, and we'll all be together soon. I love you, Richard."

"I love you too. Hurry home."

The next call was Detective Anne Bishop with the Special Victims Unit.

"Detective Bishop," she answered.

"Anne, it's Darell. I've solved your kidnapping case. There never were any kidnappers. The baby was safe the whole time with friends of the family."

Pause.

"How did you figure that out? Wait, don't tell me. You heard something from the dead woman at the séance." She laughed.

Pause.

"Darell, are you still there? How did you figure that out really?"

Darell laughed now, "You just told me not to tell you."

"Okay don't. I'm glad to hear the baby is safe, but we still have a kidnapping to address. A child was taken from her parents."

"I'm working on that," said Darell. "The mother and I are driving back from York, Pennsylvania, now. Can you meet us at the Craft house in three hours? The baby and your suspects will be there."

"Then I will be too."

"Thanks, Anne, see you soon."

HOMECOMING

ELIZABETH WAS ASLEEP ON THE FLOOR mattress with Lincoln tucked close against her. Having her home and happy went a long way towards Richard and Audrey making peace with the situation and the Millers. Audrey spoke to Michele and Michael, "I had some time to think on the ride home. I'm happy that Elizabeth is home and safe, but you came into my house in the night and stole my daughter from me."

"Audrey," Michele started, to be interrupted by Audrey's raised hand and a loud "Shush!"

"I know you thought you were doing something good, but you stole my daughter. I know the whole story now and I want to be able to accept things in faith that it must be 'one of those things that happen for a reason,' but I'm afraid acceptance of losing Elizabeth, even though she was safe, is not something that will come easy for me. Forgiveness will come even harder."

"We understand," said Michael.

"You scared us," said Richard.

Vicki and Audrey and Darell told the story of Stonehenge to Richard and Trey and the Millers. Michael and Michele told the story of Elizabeth.

Darell answered the doorbell to greet Detective Bishop. They had a conversation in the entryway.

"How do you happen to know Steven McKinney?" asked Bishop. Steven McKinney was a criminal defense attorney.

"Same fraternity freshman year at Mason."

"And how does Steven McKinney happen to know the DA?"

Darell smiled, "Same fraternity freshman year at Mason."

"I think I'm detecting a pattern here."

"They both went on to become distinguished graduates of the Antonin Scalia Law School."

"McKinney also went on to become a recent student of this particular kidnapping case."

"Really," said Darell, feigning surprise.

"He spoke with the DA about criminal defense strategy. My case is a kidnapping defined by someone taking a child from the custody of their parents. McKinney's case is that the law requires the prosecution to prove that the accused had the intent to abduct or kidnap from that custody. I would say that is proven by the act of taking the child. McKinney would say that, in this case, the intent was to protect the child from a presumed danger, thereby ensuring that the parental custody could be restored when the danger had passed."

"What does the DA say?"

"That a judge would side with McKinney."

"So, no prosecution?"

"No prosecution."

Darell smiled broadly. "Are you okay with that?"

"I have to be. I'd still like to meet with the baby and see the parents together with the alleged kidnappers to feel better about it."

"Let's go," said Darell, leading her to the chatty group in the great room.

"Most of you know Detective Bishop," he announced.

"She doesn't know Elizabeth yet," said Audrey picking the baby up and handing her to Anne. Elizabeth gurgled and smiled. Anne just smiled.

"Hello, Elizabeth. I've been looking for you, you beautiful little girl. She looks happy."

"She is," said Audrey. "She's happy to be back with her best friend Lincoln."

Michael spoke, "Detective Bishop, I want to apologize for all the trouble we caused. This is my wife, Michele. We know there are consequences for what we did, and we're ready to face whatever that is."

"Can you tell me why you wanted to take Elizabeth?"

Michele answered, "We thought she was in danger of being kidnapped. We thought if we had her and no one knew where she was, we could prevent that and keep her safe. Now we know there was no kidnapper at all."

"Audrey, how do you feel about what they did?"

"I've never been more scared than when I thought it was a real kidnapping. I know Michele loves Elizabeth and I understand what she did was meant to be good for all of us. I'd like to think things will be normal among us some day. I just don't feel that right now."

The detective turned back to the Millers. "How did you get past the dog?"

"We almost didn't," said Michael. "Lincoln barked when he first saw Michele. We were ready to give up and take off, but she was able to quiet him. We waited and no one came, so we continued."

"How did you quiet him?"

"Lincoln loves his little carrots, and I had a pocketful," said Michele.

"And I took him outside right away," said Michael. "I had picked up a long leash at the Goodwill store and tied him up at the fence where his barking wouldn't be heard in the house."

"You must have planned well," said Anne. "We didn't find any clues to go on."

"That was me," said Michael, almost proudly. "I left the car at the bend in the driveway where it couldn't be seen from the house or the road. We wore rubber doctor's gloves and old shoes with worn out soles. We weren't there for more than a minute or two after I took Lincoln out. When I was walking him out to the fence, Michele went to the nursery."

"Elizabeth helped too," said Michele. "She barely woke up and never made a sound."

"Feel better?" asked Darell of Anne.

"I still think a trial is in order." Sunken faces all around the room. "We seem to have a jury of peers already assembled. Raise your hands if anyone thinks I should handcuff Michael and Michele and take them with me now."

No hands raised.

"Then I guess my work here is done," she said, handing Elizabeth back to her mother.

Richard spoke up. "I'm angry about what happened with my daughter and the fear that Audrey and I had to live with."

"Then I should take them in?"

"No, I've known and worked with Michele and Michael since they first came to The Peacock Plume. I don't consider them criminals. I guess I just needed to say that taking someone's baby from them should have consequences regardless of the intent."

"I suspect it does," said Detective Bishop, "and I wish all of you well in working through those."

Darell walked her out to the police cruiser. "Do you think justice was served?" he asked.

"I think these are all good people caught up and confused by superstition. I also think I'll lean on you in the future when I need low friends in high places." She laughed.

"Maybe all's well that ends well."

"Do you think they learned anything from this?"

"Probably more than we'll ever know."

"Well, that's that," said Darell on returning to the group.

"So, it's over now? We can all go back to normal?" said Audrey.

"Be careful what you ask for," said Richard, smiling.

That's when Elizabeth made her loud "V" sound again.

"Just so you know," said Richard. "I looked that up. Babies aren't expected to be able to make a V sound until about twelve months."

"I'm not one of the psychics here," said Darell. "But I have a feeling Elizabeth is going to do a lot of things you don't expect in the coming years."

Vicki made the sign of the cross. "God bless us everyone."

THE END?

I doubt it.

CLOSURE

THE CRAFT HOUSEHOLD WAS WHOLE AND happy again. Lincoln was glad to have everyone back. He was still a sucker for a carrot.

Trey took Vicki off to finish their vacation, spending a lot of time in "the happiest place on Earth," conjugal bliss.

The Peacock Plume had a grand reopening. The once tired old Victorian was now a sparkling new showcase.

Darell finished his master's thesis. In the coming year he was moving into retirement from direct law enforcement and planning to hang up a shingle as a private investigator. He'd have no shortage of work thanks to his contacts through Don Weston and now Detective Anne Bishop.

"What are your thoughts on going back to the Portal?" Tom asked Vicki a month later.

"None. I don't make those kinds of plans anymore. Someone else has it all figured out, and everything happens for a reason. It's not my job to try and take the wheel of the bus. I just need to pay attention that I get off at the right stop."

"How does that feel to you?"

"Pretty peaceful, actually. Mrs. Monahan was just begin-ning to teach me about being cautious with the gift. I wonder if I would have learned that a long time ago if I hadn't lost her so soon."

"You said it yourself, everything happens for a reason. I think our work together on your recovery is done. What do you think?"

"I think it will never be done."

"Right answer! How about we keep getting together informally as creative collaborators? The article we started with on near-death experience seems to be emerging as a book with a much larger message. The experience is unusual and deeply personal. The stronger story is in moving beyond that journey and trusting one's place in those experiences. Do you agree?"

"It's a book about faith—and love."

ACKNOWLEDGMENTS

THANK YOU FOR READING 'THE PORTAL.' I'D greatly appreciate it if you could find the time to submit a review of your thoughts on the book. Genuine feedback from readers, book clubs, writer's groups, etc. gives me the confirmation and/ or direction to continually improve in this craft. Greatly appreciated!

If you are new to my writing, I welcome you. If you came here by way of 'Blame it on the Moon or 'Final Exam,' I welcome you back!

Family first, my continued thanks always to my wife, Kathy, and our dog, Mitch. It's their permission, support, and encouragement that allows me to sit at the laptop and smoke cigars for the many hours and days and months it takes for the inspirations and research to become something for a reader to enjoy. My Mom has been gone since 1989, but she was always the largest influence in my education, career, and writing. She and my late Father and the rest of the family still give me guidance, if only in my mind. Our nephew Hollywood mogul Tommy Metz III has been along for all three books giving great visual and critical advice.

Technical support for this one came from Dr. Debbie Berlin, Dr. Steele Lipe, and local pharmacist, Dr. Patel for anesthesiology and drug access. Special thanks to Debbie for the hints on ER procedure. I also reached out to a Washington DC maritime attorney very early in the process. Unfortunately, I've lost that contact info, but I hope he reads the book and recognizes my thanks.

On the professional side, I've had a wonderful opportunity over the past several years to learn from The Florida Writers Association (FWA) and the Mystery Writers of America (MWA). Thanks to my FWA mentor, Vic DiGenti, I've been blessed with hosting a monthly chapter of that organization, allowing me to regularly meet new writing contacts like Shutta Crum, my Alpha beta reader. Other authors, from novices like me to New York Times Bestsellers like John Gilstrap, have been extremely generous with their time and patience. It's an amazing community of 'Writers Helping Writers' out there.

The book construction and assembly team from 'Blame it on the Moon' and 'Final Exam' returned for 'The Portal' and I hope to work with them on the next sequel and many other works to come. That would be Editor Jennifer Ellen Cook. cover designer, Christine Holmes, and formatter, Autumn Skye. I'd never be able to competently stumble my way through publication without them.

Thanks again for your time and interest in my work!

www.ingramcontent.com/pod-product-compliance
Lightning Source LLC
Chambersburg PA
CBHW070751160726
48004CB00001B/136